Three for Show

Three
A Visua
to the

Edited by Gregory Cowar
Forest Park Community Colleg

for Show: Approach Short Story

Cindy Burns
Alex Paradowski
Lynn Wesselman

Random House
New York

First Edition
987654321
 Published in the United States by Random House, Inc., and simultaneously in Canada by Random House of Canada Limited, Toronto.

Cowan, Gregory, comp.
Three for show.

1. Short stories, American–Explication–Audio-visual aids. 2. Short stories, English–Explication–Audio-visual aids. 3. Short stories, American. 4. Short stories, English. I. Title.
PS374.S5C6 823'.01 72-12512
ISBN 0-394-31089-6

Manufactured in the United States of America. Composed by Universal Graphics, Maple Shade, N.J. Printed and bound by Von Hoffman Press, St. Louis, Missouri.

Permissions Acknowledgments

JOHN BARTH, "Frame-Tale" from *Lost in the Funhouse* by John Barth. Copyright © 1963, 1966, 1968, 1969 by John Barth. Reprinted by permission of Doubleday & Company, Inc.

STEPHEN CRANE, "The Bride Comes to Yellow Sky" from *An Omnibus* by Stephen Crane. Reprinted by permission of Alfred A. Knopf, Inc.

GEORGE DAVIS, "Coming Home" from *Amistad I*, edited by John A. Williams and Charles F. Harris. Copyright © 1970 by John A. Williams and Charles F. Harris. Reprinted by permission of Random House, Inc.

E. M. FORSTER, "The Celestial Omnibus" from *The Collected Tales of E. M. Forster* by E. M. Forster. Published 1947 by Alfred A. Knopf, Inc. Reprinted by permission of Alfred A. Knopf, Inc., and Sidgwick & Jackson, Ltd.

LANGSTON HUGHES, "Coffee Break" from *Simple's Uncle Sam* by Langston Hughes. Copyright © 1965 by Langston Hughes. Reprinted by permission of Hill and Wang, a division of Farrar, Straus & Giroux, Inc.

KRISTIN HUNTER, "An Interesting Social Study." Copyright 1967 by Kristin Hunter. Reprinted by permission of Harold Matson Company, Inc.

JAMES JOYCE, "Counterparts" from *Dubliners* by James Joyce. Copyright © 1967 by The Estate of James Joyce. All rights reserved. Originally published by B. W. Huebsch, Inc. Reprinted by permission of The Viking Press, Inc.

R. J. MEADDOUGH III, "The Death of Tommy Grimes" from *The Best Short Stories by Negro Writers*, edited by Langston Hughes. Reprinted by permission of the author.

JOYCE CAROL OATES, "The Loves of Franklin Ambrose." Copyright © 1971 by Joyce Carol Oates. Copyright © 1972 by Joyce Carol Oates. Originally appeared in *Playboy* magazine. Reprinted by permission of the author and Blanche C. Gregory, Inc.

DOROTHY PARKER, "Arrangement in Black and White" from *The Portable Dorothy Parker.* Copyright 1927, © 1955 by Dorothy Parker. Originally appeared in *The New Yorker.* Reprinted by permission of The Viking Press, Inc.

JOHN STEINBECK, "The Chrysanthemums" from *The Long Valley* by John Steinbeck. Copyright 1937, © renewed 1965 by John Steinbeck. Reprinted by permission of The Viking Press, Inc.

JAMES THURBER, "A Couple of Hamburgers" from *The Thurber Carnival* by James Thurber. Copyright © 1945 James Thurber. Originally appeared in *The New Yorker.* Reprinted by permission.

JOHN UPDIKE, "A & P" from *Pigeon Feathers and Other Stories* by John Updike. Copyright © 1962 by John Updike. Originally appeared in *The New Yorker.* Reprinted by permission of Alfred A. Knopf, Inc.

KURT VONNEGUT, JR., "Harrison Bergeron" from *Welcome to the Monkey House* by Kurt Vonnegut, Jr. Copyright © 1961 by Kurt Vonnegut, Jr. Originally appeared in *Fantasy and Science Fiction.* Reprinted by permission of Delacorte Press.

JOHN A. WILLIAMS, "Son in the Afternoon." Reprinted by permission of the author.

WILLIAM CARLOS WILLIAMS, "The Use of Force" from *The Farmers' Daughters* by William Carlos Williams. Copyright 1938 by William Carlos Williams. Reprinted by permission of New Directions Publishing Corporation.

We also gratefully acknowledge the following:

The Great Atlantic & Pacific Tea Company, Inc., for permission to use the A&P shopping bag on p. 1.

Sunshine Biscuits, Inc., for permission to use an illustration of HiHo Crackers on p. 2.

Appleseed Music, Inc., for permission to reprint "I Ain't a-Marchin' Any More," by Phil Ochs, on p. 21. © Copyright 1964 by Appleseed Music, Inc. All rights reserved.

Acknowledgments

Many people contributed to the making of this book. In order of appearance, they are:

The students of Introduction to Literature, section 01, Spring Semester, 1970. Steve Betts, Larry Blue, Cynthia (Cindy) Burns, Ronald Carr, Carolyn Clay, Paula Dorn, Roberta Elfrink, Ray Ellerbeck, Marvin Feldman, Sharon Fortner, Tom Garcia, Betsy Gordon, Elaine Herman, Joseph Hoeing, Celestine (Jay) Hughes, Laverne Ivery, Chester Jakubowicz, Darlene Johnson, Nancy Kurth, Chris Licata, Arlene Mitchell, Charles Mitchell, Dean Muchnick, Ed Mueller, Alex Paradowski, William Pullen, Stephen Reynolds, Theresa Riordan, Marilyn Sinak, Margaret Smith, Art Vasterling, Lynn Wesselman, James Williams, Special oakleaf clusters for Jay, Darlene, and Chris.

William Sparke and Clark McKowen, whose book, *Montage*, taught us a lot. (Clark McKowen even took a personal interest, looking at some of the early materials, writing letters of encouragement, and, once, sending some valentines.)

Sue Cowan, Greg's wife, who not only put up with our mess in the dining room and our noise and late hours, but even made us feel comfortable and welcome.

Betty Paradowski, Alex's wife, who provided food and shelter, while Alex and Greg worked round the clock one weekend.

Judy Rosenberg, editor at Random House, who helped us select some of the stories; and June Fischbein, editor at Random House, who helped with the final preparation of the manuscript.

Jim Smith, English editor at Random House, who signed the contract for this unusual book and—look—he published it!

Elizabeth Wooten, Cleveland Community College, Myrna Harrison, Laney College, and Elisabeth McPherson, Forest Park Community College, who read the finished manuscript perceptively and sympathetically, offering constructive suggestions that improved it.

Finally, Dick Friedrich, chairman of the English department, and Joel Margulis, chairman of the Humanities Division—two people who help to make Forest Park Community College the kind of place where things like this can happen.

Contents

Introduction

This book began the day I stopped teaching. It grew out of a class listed in the college catalog as "Introduction to Fiction: Short Story and Novel." The thirty-five students were mostly sophomores and represented a fair cross section of the campus population in age, interest, academic major, and previous experience with literature. Some of them read a lot, some didn't. Many hadn't taken a college literature course before.

During the first three weeks we read several stories and had rather free and general discussions about them. We were getting along reasonably well. Then it came time to deal with the traditional aspects of the course—to talk, as we were "spozed to," about theme, symbols, characterization, setting, plot, point of view, and so on. Instead of working together, the class separated—no longer "we," but "I" and "they." "I" lectured at them about techniques and effects; "they" slept, whispered, read, worked math problems, wrote letters, or just sat looking stunned and comotose. We were up against the same old dilemma: a discussion conducted in abstract and unreal jargon was destroying whatever pleasure we originally had in the stories. Yet I was convinced (and still am) that an enlarged understanding of what a writer does and the way he does it leads to deepened pleasure.

I agreed with McLuhan that most people today respond more readily and fully to presentational than to linear communication, but I couldn't get beyond the notion that literature is essentially linear. The very nature of print makes linearity inevitable—words stretch out, one after another on a line that goes on and on. The nature of actual experience, however—and to a lesser extent, film and television—is presentational: we are simultaneously presented with a mass of impressions, colors, shapes, movements, and sounds—all of which contribute to effect and meaning. But even though literature is linear, its effect, for sophisticated readers, is cumulative: the words, sentences, and paragraphs add up to a total greater than the sum of the parts. I knew my job as a literature teacher was to help students see and appreciate that cumulative effect, to help them react to short stories as quickly and perceptively as they react to film. But, because I had been schooled in writing about writing, it didn't occur to me that I could explain about words and sentences without using more words and sentences, without in effect, piling linear on linear.

The combination of McLuhan and those slumbering students kept nagging at me. Wasn't there some way of getting students to see what really went on in a story without using critical terminology, without lecturing, without assigning essays on so-and-so's symbolic use of color? In other words, wasn't there some way to get out of the linear into the presentational mode?

When the class was at its dullest—even the letter writers had gone to sleep—I received an examination copy of an unconventional book, a composition text that came to grips with the problem that puzzled me. The authors were experimenting with visual devices that led readers to expand their perception beyond the written line. Color made main points spring out from the page; variations in type emphasized variations in points of view; overprinting and design connected one idea with another; repetition of color, print, and design carried a key concept all through a section. Visually oriented readers couldn't avoid "seeing" what the print said. Linear communication had not quite become presentational—between book covers it can never quite do that—but it had gone a long way toward it.

I was excited. I took the book into class and asked my dozing students what they thought. The response was electric. Everybody woke up, asked swarms of questions, offered swarms of answers. Soon somebody noticed that, although the book contained a few short stories, they had all been printed "straight," without visuals, and somebody else asked why. The answer took a week of talking, in which I played a relatively minor role, but during that week the students took themselves deeper into the nature of fiction than any lecture of mine could ever have taken them. In the discussion, one faction maintained that good literature deals with concepts and that concepts can indeed be dealt with presentationally; therefore, short stories can be explained and understood in a presentational mode. Another, more traditional, faction insisted that out of respect for the writer's medium, words, one ought not to tamper by mixing in other media.

Both factions appealed to me to arbitrate, but it was more than I could handle. I could only suggest that literary criticism is a kind of explication, and although that explication has traditionally been done in words, there was no real reason it couldn't be done visually—except that I didn't know how to do it.

Conversation whirled up again, some students maintaining that pictures merely *illustrated* content, like a first-grade book that shows a picture of a shoe just above S-H-O-E. But after another week, there was a consensus that illustrations were one thing, *explications* something else. Illustrations merely illustrated; explications showed how the story "worked," not just by showing the object described, but by showing why the description mattered. Explications were visuals that led to deeper understanding. To prove that point, they asked if they could take one short story, have each student pick a passage and design a visual explication, and talk about those explications during the next class. "Why not?" said I, and they did.

The process of selecting a passage caused the students to read very closely. Figuring out how the passage could be visually explicated, not just illustrated, led to a deliberate consideration of meaning. That next class meeting witnessed a good deal of dispute about what a given passage "really" meant, and whether a given visual was "really" an explication or merely an illustration. The student who had used the printing on an A & P sack (see page 1) for the title page of John Updike's *A & P* said he was just doing it for fun, enjoying the fact that there was an actual A & P, as well as a fictional one. Somebody objected because the printing on the bag said "we care," whereas the point of Updike's story was that the store did not "care." Then everybody got into the act, some of them claiming that A & P cared, all right, but about different things, and *that* was the point of the story. "Of course they don't care," another student said. "That's what makes the paper bag so nice." Without any mention of "irony," everybody seemed to have grasped the ironic intent.

Another drawing brought in that day showed bare footprints on the tile floor (see page 5). "Illustration!" the class shouted, but the woman who brought it said no. "Obviously the soft outlines of the foot contrast with the starkly rigid line of the tiles, as anybody with an eye in his head could see. The footprints are people–human values–and the hard tiles are the store's attitude, and *that*'s what the story is *about*." I kept out of it. The students were involved with the story and with each other, and though a chance passerby might have thought the room was in utter chaos, it was obvious to all of us insiders that some very serious learning was taking place.

After that my lecture on image and allusion seemed redundant; I threw it out the window. The students went on to more passages in more stories. Soon the class had divided itself into groups of five or six, each group working as a committee to select a single story, explicate it visually, and present it to the rest of the class. I didn't have to talk about allusions. When R. J. Meaddough says, at the end of *The Death of Tommy Grimes*, that it was "like the tolling of the bell," a student was right there with John Donne's line from "Meditation 17": "Any man's death diminishes me because I am involved in mankind, and therefore never send to know for whom the bell tolls; it tolls for thee." The title of the story took on a clearer meaning–the bell tolled for Tommy Grimes; part of what made him human had died in his responsibility for another human's death.

There was no stopping that class. Symbols showed up on the page. Points of view became visible. Theme stood out from plot. The students were determined to understand exactly what the author had done and insisted on explaining their ideas until the whole class understood that interpretation, whether or not everybody agreed with it. I wasn't the teacher–everybody was. We were all learning and astonished that we were learning so much, so intensely.

Even more important, we were all enjoying ourselves. The stories we worked on were not dead, but very much alive. And the students were reading more stories on their own. Without anybody putting it into words, we had demonstrated what all sensitive readers subconsciously do: visualize as they read. We had also discovered how necessary that visualization is, not only to comprehension but to analysis. What the students were doing as they created their visual explications was to take both those steps, visualization and analysis; but, instead of verbalizing their analysis, they *showed* it. They began with the linear, as any reader must, but they transformed it, through their own imaginative approach, to a presentational "discussion" that clarified and illumined–without any critical literary terms at all.

Like anybody excited about a discovery, the students wanted a broader field for their teaching. They had already taught me a good deal–showing me things I hadn't "seen" in the stories before. Five students, working as a group on Steinbeck's *The Chrysanthemums*, did an explication of the beginning of that story, showing the mountains in the shape of a pot and above them a lid made out of the words, "like a lid." Although I must have read that story fifteen times over the last five years, it was the first time I "saw" the pot imagery in that passage.

But the students wanted a larger audience than I represented; they wanted to share with lots of people what they had seen in the stories and the way they had seen it: they wanted to publish a book. So they did. This is it.

The first three stories in the book include the explications that our class produced. These first stories are accompanied by "critical essays," and, just as some readers disagree with the interpretation one critic gives a story, so some of you will disagree with our interpretations. We have shown the stories as we see them; we hope your discussions about our way of seeing will be both specific and lively. After all, the aim of a literature class is not to insist that everybody agree, either with the teacher or each other; the aim is to discover what you think, and why.

The thirteen unexplicated stories are for you to visualize, to explicate, to argue over. You can, of course, do your explicating at home alone, but we think you'll find, as we did, that working in groups is more fun. Ideas bounce off other ideas, and the abrasion helps to smooth them out. Part of the excitement our class found was in the doing, part of it in the sharing. But whatever system you use for your explications, the process of "seeing" these stories for yourself should help you become deeper, more sympathetic, more sophisticated readers;

it should increase your enjoyment of what you read. Without using any traditional terminology, you can develop your own standards of criticism, and if you want the terminology later on, you can pick it up easily enough.

Some of the stories in this book are "standard"—lots of people have read and talked about them during the last twenty or thirty years. Some of them will be new, both to you and to your teacher. All of them have been chosen for several reasons: first, they are strong and energetic; second, they represent a wide cross section of human experience—black and white, male and female; and third, their themes, their symbols, and their tensions are especially well-suited to this kind of "seeing."

If the visuals you produce are not as professional looking as the ones you see here, that doesn't matter. The learning is in the process, the doing, not in the polished product. When our class decided to attempt a book, it was clear that for publication the visuals would have to be much more finished than was necessary for class. And although nearly everybody in the class wanted a book published, not everybody had the time, the energy, or the special skills to deal with problems of layout, color, design, pagination—concerns far removed from the reading and understanding of fiction.

So, when a group began to meet twice a week at my house, often from eight in the evening until three in the morning, only about ten or twelve students from the class came. What we started with was artistically crude. Drawings in crayon by people who had never drawn before and pictures torn from magazines had served to get the ideas across to the class, but we didn't think they would meet publication standards. The three stories as they are shown here represent hours of refining and polishing the first ideas.

Actually, we explicated more stories than appear in this book, and we were more successful with some than with others. This kind of "seeing" works better on some stories. We spent hour after hour, for example, on Faulkner's *Barn Burning* and were never pleased with the results. Our presentational ingenuity was no match for Faulkner's linear mastery, but even though we didn't succeed, the trying taught us more about Faulkner's technique than we could have learned in any other way.

As the year wore on, the pressures of other obligations, both personal and academic, forced several people to dropout of the evening workshops. Charles Mitchell and Ronald Carr were among the five students who came most regularly and worked the longest, but they had to withdraw before the project was quite finished. The three students whose names appear on the cover, therefore, are mainly responsible for the finished forms of these visuals, although the ideas behind them and the excitement involved in the process belong to the whole class.

Gregory M. Cowan
St. Louis, Missouri

Three for Show

A&P

John Updike

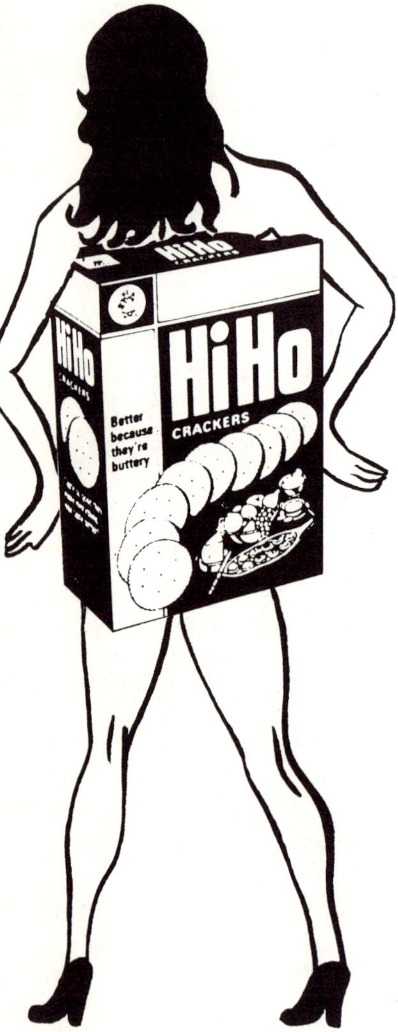

In walks these three girls in nothing but bathing suits. I'm in the third checkout slot, with my back to the door, so I don't see them until they're over by the bread. The one that caught my eye first was the one in the plaid green two-piece. She was a chunky kid, with a good tan and a sweet broad soft-looking can with those two crescents of white just under it, where the sun never seems to hit, at the top of the backs of her legs. I stood there with my hand on a box of Hi-Ho crackers trying to remember if I rang it up or not. I ring it up again and the customer starts giving me hell. She's one of these cash-register-watchers, a witch about fifty with rouge on her cheekbones and no eyebrows, and I know it made her day to trip me up. She'd been watching cash registers for fifty years and probably never seen a mistake before.

By the time I got her feathers smoothed and her goodies into a bag—she gives me a little snort in passing, if she'd been born at the right time they would have burned her over in Salem—by the time I get her on her way the girls had circled around the bread and were coming back, without a pushcart, back my way along the counters, in the aisle between the checkout and the Special bins. They didn't even have shoes on. There was this chunky one, with the two-piece—it was bright green and the seams on the bra were still sharp and her belly was still pretty pale so I guessed she just got it (the suit)—there was this one, with one of those chubby berry-faces, the lips all bunched together under her nose, this one, and

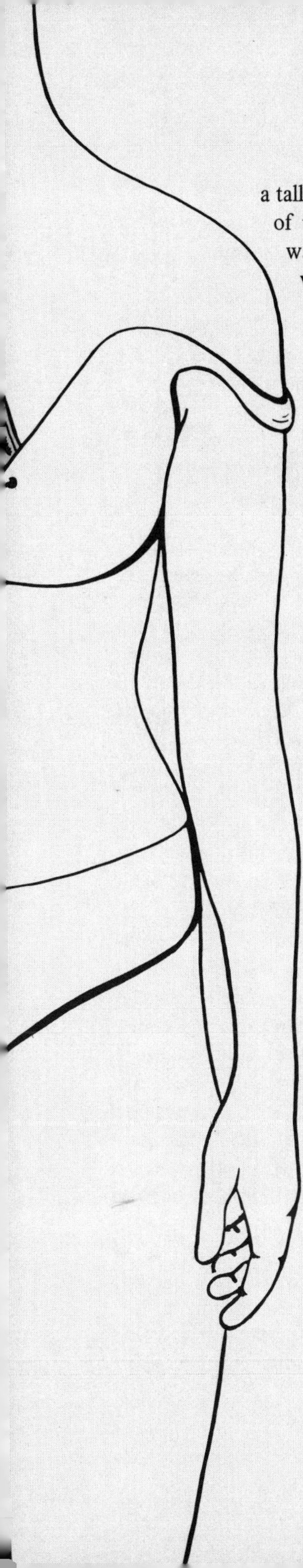

a tall one, with black hair that hadn't quite frizzed right, and one of these sunburns right across under the eyes, and a chin that was too long—you know, the kind of girl other girls think is very "striking," and "attractive" but never quite makes it, as they very well know, which is why they like her so much—and then the third one, that wasn't quite so tall. She was the queen. She kind of led them, the other two peeking around and making their shoulders round. She didn't look around, not this queen, she just walked straight on slowly, on these long white prima-donna legs. She came down a little hard on her heels, as if she didn't walk in her bare feet that much, putting down her heels and then letting the weight move along to her toes as if she was testing the floor with every step, putting a little deliberate extra action into it. You never know for sure how girls' minds work (do you really think it's a mind in there or just a little buzz like a bee in a glass jar?) but you got the idea she had talked the other two into coming in here with her, and now she was showing them how to do it, walk slow and hold yourself straight.

She had on a kind of dirty-pink—beige maybe, I don't know—bathing suit with a little nubble all over it and, what got me, the straps were down. They were off her shoulders looped loose around the cool tops of her arms, and I guess as a result the suit had slipped a little on her, so all around the top of the cloth there was this shining rim. If it hadn't been there you wouldn't have known there could have been anything whiter than those shoulders. With the straps pushed off, there was nothing between the top of the suit and the top of her head except just *her*, this clean bare plane of the top of her chest down from the shoulder bones like a dented sheet of metal tilted in the light. I mean, it was more than pretty.

She had sort of oaky hair that the sun and salt had bleached, done up in a bun that was unravelling, and a kind of prim face. Walking into the A & P with your straps down, I suppose it's the only kind of face you *can* have. She held her head so high her neck, coming up out of those white shoulders, looked kind of stretched, but I didn't mind. The longer her neck was, the more of her there was.

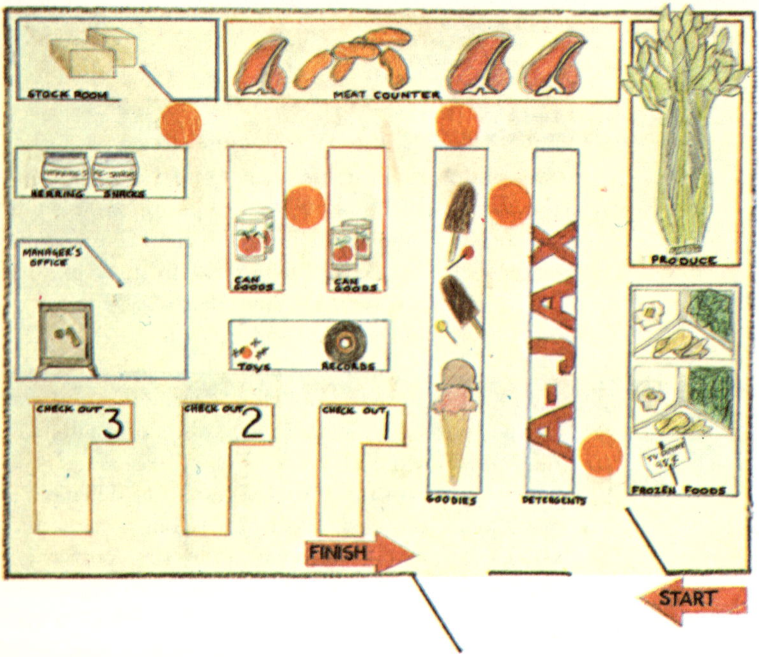

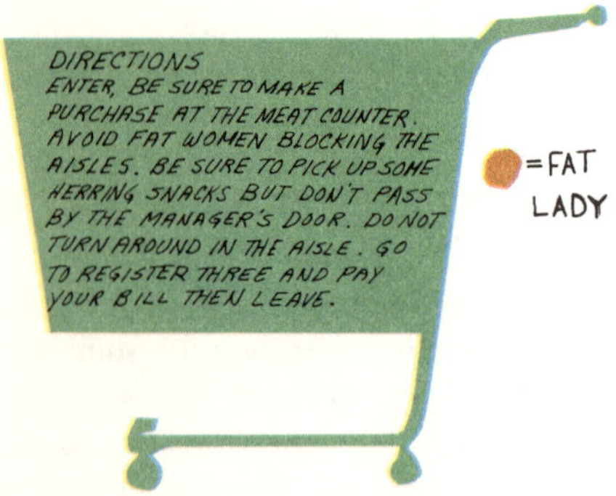

She must have felt in the corner of her eye me and over my shoulder Stokesie in the second slot watching, but she didn't tip. Not this queen. She kept her eyes moving across the racks, and stopped, and turned so slow it made my stomach rub the inside of my apron, and buzzed to the other two, who kind of huddled against her for relief, and then they all three of them went up the cat - and - dog - food - breakfast - cereal - macaroni - rice - raisins - seasonings - spreads - spaghetti - soft - drinks - crackers - and - cookies aisle. From the third slot I look straight up this aisle to the meat counter, and I watched them all the way. The fat one with the tan sort of fumbled with the cookies, but on second thought she put the package back. The sheep pushing their carts down the aisle—the girls were walking against the usual traffic (not that we have one-way signs or anything)—were pretty hilarious. You could see them, when Queenie's white shoulders dawned on them, kind of jerk, or hop, or hiccup, but their eyes snapped back to their own baskets and on they pushed. I bet you could set off dynamite in an A & P and the people would by and large keep reaching and checking oatmeal off their lists and muttering "Let me see, there was a third thing, began with A, asparagus, no, ah, yes, applesauce!" or whatever it is they do mutter. But there was no doubt, this jiggled them. A few houseslaves in pin curlers even looked around after pushing their carts past to make sure what they had seen was correct.

You know, it's one thing to have a girl in a bathing suit down on the beach, where what with the glare nobody can look at each other much anyway, and another thing in the cool of the A & P, under the fluorescent lights, against all those stacked packages, with her feet paddling along naked over our checkerboard green-and-cream rubber-tile floor.

"Oh Daddy," Stokesie said beside me. "I feel so faint."

"Darling," I said. "Hold me tight." Stokesie's married, with two babies chalked up on his fuselage already, but as far as I can tell that's the only difference. He's twenty-two, and I was nineteen this April.

"Is it done?" he asks, the responsible married man finding his voice. I forgot to say he thinks he's going to be manager some sunny day, maybe in 1990 when it's called the Great Alexandrov and Petrooshki Tea Company or something.

What he meant was, our town is five miles from a beach, with a big summer colony out on the Point, but

we're right in the middle of town, and the women generally put on a shirt or shorts or something before they get out of the car into the street. And anyway these are usually women with six children and varicose veins mapping their legs and nobody, including them, could care less. As I say,

we're right in the middle of town, and if you stand at our front doors you can see two banks and the Congregational church and the newspaper store and three real-estate offices and about twenty-seven old freeloaders tearing up Central Street because the sewer broke again. It's not as if we're on the Cape; we're north of Boston and there's people in this town haven't seen the ocean for twenty years.

The girls had reached the meat counter and were asking McMahon something. He pointed, they pointed, and they shuffled out of sight behind a pyramid of Diet Delight peaches. All that was left for us to see was old McMahon patting his mouth and looking after them sizing up their joints. Poor kids, I began to feel sorry for them, they couldn't help it.

FRESH MEATS

Now here comes the sad part of the story, at least my family says it's sad, but I don't think it's so sad myself. The store's pretty empty, it being Thursday afternoon, so there was nothing much to do except lean on the register and wait for the girls to show up again. The whole store was like a pinball machine and I didn't know which tunnel they'd come out of. After a while they come around out of the far aisle, around the light bulbs, records at discount of the Caribbean Six or Tony Martin Sings or some such gunk you wonder they waste the wax on, sixpacks of candy bars, and plastic toys done up in cellophane that fall apart when a kid looks at them anyway. Around they come, Queenie still leading the way, and holding a little gray jar in her hand. Slots Three through Seven are unmanned and I could see her wondering between Stokes and me, but Stokesie with his usual luck draws an old party in baggy gray pants who stumbles up with four giant cans of pineapple juice (what do these bums *do* with all that pineapple juice? I've often asked myself) so the girls come to me. Queenie puts down the jar and I take it into my fingers icy cold. Kingfish Fancy Herring Snacks in Pure Sour Cream: 49¢. Now her hands are empty, not a ring or a bracelet, bare as God made them, and I wonder where the money's coming from. Still with that prim look she lifts a folded dollar bill out of the hollow at the center of her nubbled pink top. The jar went heavy in my hand. Really, I thought that was so cute.

Then everybody's luck begins to run out. Lengel comes in from haggling with a truck full of cabbages on the lot and is about to scuttle into that door marked MANAGER behind which he hides all day when the girls touch his eye. Lengel's pretty dreary, teaches Sunday school and the rest, but he doesn't miss much. He comes over and says, "Girls, this isn't the beach."

Queenie blushes, though maybe it's just a brush of sunburn I was noticing for the first time, now that she was so close. "My mother asked me to pick up a jar of herring snacks." Her voice kind of startled me, the way voices do when you see the people first, coming out so flat and dumb yet kind of tony, too, the way it ticked over "pick up" and "snacks." All of a sudden I slid right down her voice into her living room. Her father and the other men were standing around in ice-cream coats and bow ties and the women were in sandals picking up herring snacks on toothpicks off a big glass plate and they were all holding drinks the color of water with olives and sprigs of mint in them. When my parents have somebody over they get lemonade and if it's a real racy affair Schlitz in tall glasses with "They'll Do It Every Time" cartoons stencilled on.

"That's all right," Lengel said. "But this isn't the beach." His repeating this struck me as funny, as if it had just occurred to him, and he had been thinking all these years the A&P was a great big dune and he was the head lifeguard. He didn't like my smiling—as I say he doesn't miss much—but he concentrates on giving the girls that sad Sunday-school-superintendent stare.

Queenie's blush is no sunburn now, and the plump one in plaid, that I liked better from the back—a really sweet can—pipes up, "We weren't doing any shopping. We just came in for the one thing."

"That makes no difference," Lengel tells her, and I could see from the way his eyes went that he hadn't noticed she was wearing a two-piece before. "We want you decently dressed when you come in here."

"We *are* decent," Queenie says suddenly, her lower lip pushing, getting sore now that she remembers her place, a place from which the crowd that runs the A&P must look pretty crummy. Fancy Herring Snacks flashed in her very blue eyes.

"Girls, I don't want to argue with you. After this come in here with your shoulders covered. It's our policy." He turns his back. That's policy for you. Policy is what the kingpins want. What the others want is juvenile delinquency.

All this while, the customers had been showing up with their carts but, you know, sheep, seeing a scene, they had all bunched up on Stokesie, who shook open a paper bag as gently as peeling a peach, not wanting to miss a word. I could feel in the silence everybody getting nervous, most of all Lengel, who asks me, "Sammy, have you rung up their purchase?"

I thought and said "No" but it wasn't about that I was thinking. I go through the punches, 4, 9, GROC, TOT–it's more complicated than you think, and after you do it often enough, it begins to make a little song, that you hear words to, in my case "Hello (*bing*) there, you (*gung*) hap-py *pee*-pul (*splat*)!"–the *splat* being the drawer flying out. I uncrease the bill, tenderly as you may imagine, it just having come from between the two smoothest scoops of vanilla I had ever known were there, and pass a half and a penny into her narrow pink palm, and nestle the herrings in a bag and twist its neck and hand it over, all the time thinking.

The girls, and who'd blame them, are in a hurry to get out, so I say "I quit" to Lengel

quick enough for them to hear, hoping they'll stop and watch me, their unsuspected hero. They keep right on going, into the electric eye; the door flies open and they flicker across the lot to their car, Queenie and Plaid and Big Tall Goony-Goony (not that as raw material she was so bad), leaving me with Lengel and a kink in his eyebrow.

"Did you say something, Sammy?"

"I said I quit."

"I thought you did."

"You didn't have to embarrass them."

"It was they who were embarrassing us."

I started to say something that came out "Fiddle de-doo." It's a saying of my grandmother's, and I know she would have been pleased.

"I don't think you know what you're saying," Lengel said.

"I know you don't." I said. "But I do." I pull the bow at the back of my apron and start shrugging it off my shoulders. A couple customers that had been heading for my slot begin to knock against each other, like scared pigs in a chute.

Lengel sighs and begins to look very patient and old and gray. He's been a friend of my parents for years. "Sammy, you don't want to do this to your Mom and Dad," he tells me. It's true, I don't. But it seems to me that once you begin a gesture it's fatal not to go through with it. I fold the apron, "Sammy" stitched in red on the pocket, and put it on the counter, and drop the bow tie on top of it. The bow tie is theirs, if you've ever wondered. "You'll feel this for the rest of your life," Lengel says, and I know that's true, too, but remembering how he made that pretty girl blush makes me so scrunchy inside I punch the No Sale tab and the machine whirs "pee-pul" and the drawer splats out. One advantage to this scene taking place in summer, I can follow this up with a clean exit, there's no fumbling around getting your coat and galoshes, I just saunter into the electric eye in my white shirt that my mother ironed the night before, and the door heaves itself open, and outside the sunshine is skating around on the asphalt.

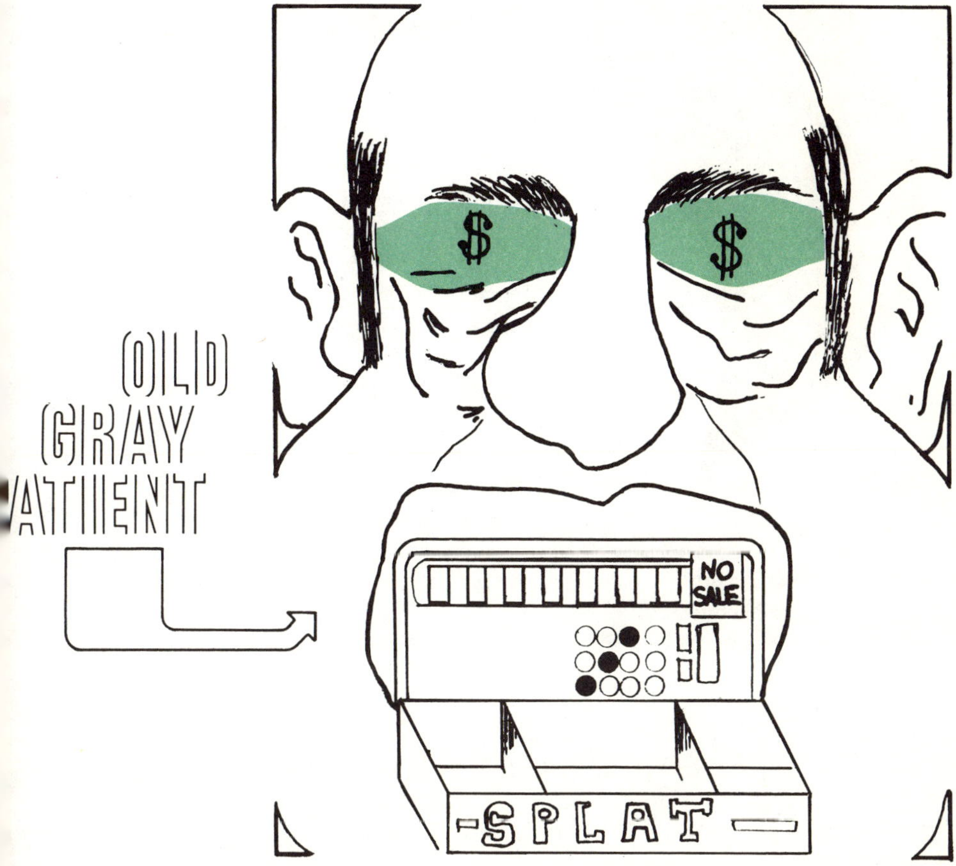

I look around for my girls, but they're gone, of course. There wasn't anybody but some young married screaming with her children about some candy they didn't get by the door of a powder-blue Falcon station wagon. Looking back in the big windows, over the bags of peat moss and aluminum lawn furniture stacked on the pavement, I could see Lengel in my place in the slot, checking the sheep through. His face was dark gray and his back stiff, as if he'd just had an injection of iron, and my stomach kind of fell as I felt how hard the world was going to be to me hereafter.

... as I felt how hard the world was going to be to me hereafter.

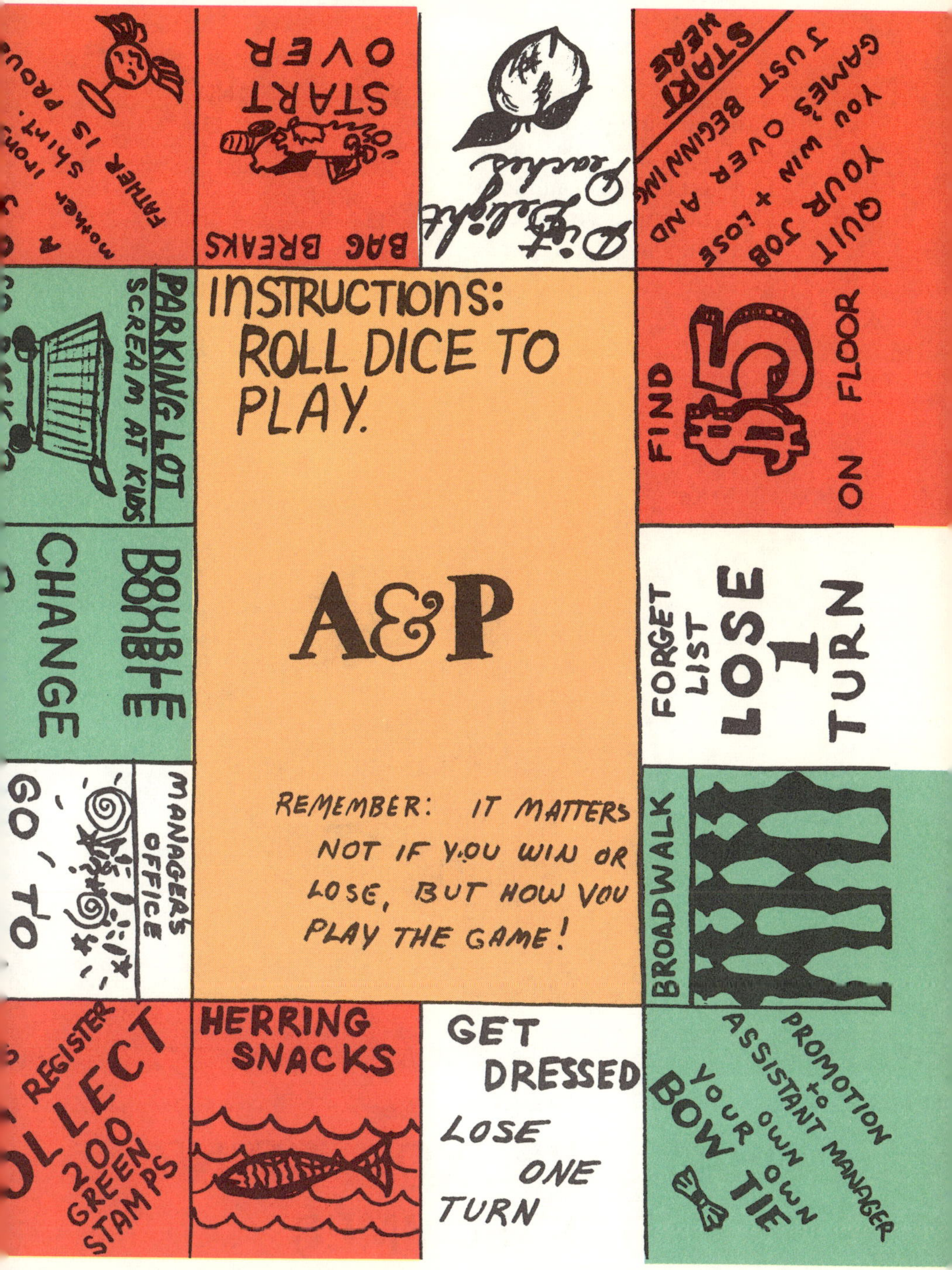

INSTRUCTIONS:
ROLL DICE TO PLAY.
A&P
REMEMBER: IT MATTERS NOT IF YOU WIN OR LOSE, BUT HOW YOU PLAY THE GAME!
START HERE
QUIT YOUR JOB + LOSE AND YOU WIN OVER AND GAME'S JUST BEGINNING
FIND $5 ON FLOOR
FORGET LIST LOSE 1 TURN
BROADWALK
PROMOTION to ASSISTANT MANAGER YOUR OWN OWN BOW TIE
GET DRESSED
LOSE ONE TURN
HERRING SNACKS
REGISTER
COLLECT 200 GREEN STAMPS
GO TO MANAGER'S OFFICE
BUBBLE CHANGE
PARKING LOT
SCREAM AT KIDS
BAG BREAKS
START OVER

	YES	NO
Can you win by quitting?	☐	☐
Can you quit by winning?	☐	☐
Can you both win and lose?	☐	☐
Can you quit if you win?	☐	☐
Can you play if you quit?	☐	☐

What do you mean by–
a) win
b) lose
c) play
d) quit

WHAT ARE <u>YOU</u> DOING THIS SUMMER

THE DEATH of TOMMY GRIMES
I wanna tell you my boy became a man today

The Death of Tommy Grimes

R. J. Meaddough III

Tommy had become part of the ground. At least he felt that way as he watched the dew and the daylight make giant shiny cobwebs of the treetops. The sun had not yet risen and a mist lay over the ground, which made the forest seem rather spooky to him.

His nose itched and he longed to scratch it, maybe just nudge it a little, but Pa said don't move, don't twitch, don't even breathe hard. Not one arm, one hand, even one finger, he said. "He knows the woods," Pa told him; "you'll never know he's there; suddenly he'll just *be* there looking at you, just looking."

It started so long ago, Tommy remembered, almost a year, when he was just eleven. That night, in the hen-yard, with the weasel's eyes glistening in the flashlight. He never even fired a shot, just stood there with his mouth open, foolish, while the weasel dashed into the woods. And Pa knocking the rifle from his hands and asking, "Why didn't you shoot? What you waiting on? What's wrong with you, boy?" "Pa, I . . . I couldn't, Pa. I just couldn't." Pa hunkered down and pulled on a blade of grass. He didn't say anything for a minute, just knelt there chewing on that grass. "You never did like to kill nothing did you, boy? Even when you was small." Tommy looked at the ground without saying anything and his father sighed, "Tommy, dammit a man always dies a little when he kills something, but it just plain has to be done. Some animals just ain't no damn good and got to be killed. Understand?"

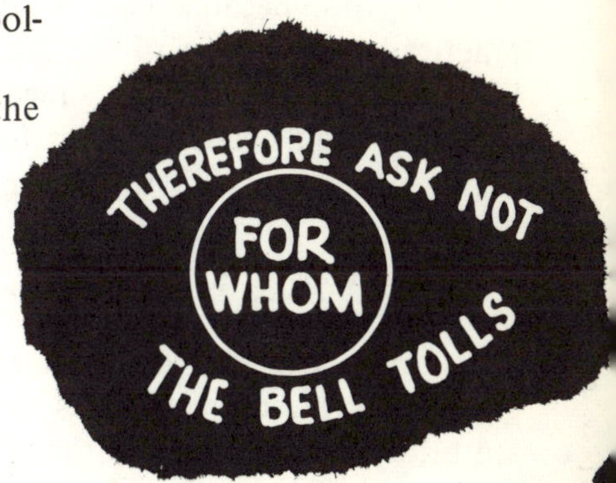

He nodded without answering, still looking at the ground, and Pa stood up with a groan and they walked into the hen-house without speaking. They counted forty-three dead pullets, lying in red and white patches of feathers, blood, and confusion.

So he began to practice with the rifle, shooting at moving targets, and the rifle became part of his arm. It seemed so long that Pa practiced with him, so long. Again and again he would take a deep breath, let some out, then squeeze the trigger. So long, so very long.

Tommy felt beads of sweat form on his forehead despite the chill that remained in the forest air. Soon the beads would form into droplets and run down his face and burn his eyes. There was a handkerchief in his coat pocket just a few inches away but he could not, dare not reach for it. But soon it would be over. Soon.

It got so that he could hit anything he aimed at, even things a good bit out. And sometimes, when he turned real quick, he would see pride in Pa's eyes. But then Pa would always make his face blank and say, "We-e-ell, Tommy," real grim-like, "you're getting better but you need more practice."

Pa taught him how to track animals and how to lead quail, and how to lean into the rifle to take up the recoil. And Pa showed him how to lie quiet so the forest forgot he was there and Nature went on about her business.

And the time came last night when Pa came home and mentioned that some of the men were going into the forest to get a buck; and how it might be some good shooting because bucks were fast, real fast.

He bent his head to eat his beans, yet he knew without looking that his father was watching him, way out of the corner of his eye. He knew, too, that Pa wouldn't have said a word if Ma was there—she was always saying he was too young for something or other—but she was visiting overnight up in Colliersville. And he thought how it must be for Pa when the other men bragged about their boys, and him so scared to kill a weasel, and he knew what he had to do.

"Pa," he murmured, "think maybe I could go a time at that old buck?"

"Boy, this ain't no old buck, it's a young one," Pa said, making like he was surprised. "Boy, you might get hurt."

"Some time, I think I'd like to take my turn," he answered, face even closer to the beans.

"Well I'll think about it, boy," Pa mumbled, but he couldn't hide a gleam in his eye.

Tommy slowly, ever so slowly, rubbed his forehead along his sleeve and watched the gloom in front of him. Somewhere out there Pa had circled around and was trampling through the woods, scaring everything away, away toward the clearing where he lay waiting.

He laughed in his mind when he thought of the last time when Pa had gone down to the Hut for a drink with the "boys," as he called them. And when he came out his eyes were gleaming like the mischief and he wobbled into the yard like he didn't know how to walk. He had gone downstairs in his pajamas and they sat on the back porch and listened to the crickets and looked at the stars. Maybe afterwards Pa would let him go into the Hut and talk with the men and drink liquor. But right then he had to be satisfied with listening to Pa tell stories that he had heard at the Hut and then squeeze his arm at the end and laugh, oh my, how he would laugh. Then he filled his pipe and stared out across the backyard toward the north pasture.

"Dawn in the forest is a beautiful thing, boy, beautiful. All the colors and wild flowers, fresh streams, cool breeze, you feel life, boy, feel it! Even though there ain't a sound you feel it. You see a flash of white and you know some rabbit's going home. Or you might see a chuck burrowing in. And the trees," he whispered, "they just stand there watching you. Been there before you came, be there after you gone."

"Gee, Pa," he murmured, "you make it sound so nice I don't know's I want to *hunt* tomorrow."

Pa smiled. "It *is* nice, boy, real nice, but things got to be done to keep it that way. Fox eats a rabbit, he keeps the rabbit population down, else they'd overrun the land. Same here. You hunt 'cause you hungry and got to eat, that's one reason. Then you might hunt for the sport–pit your mind against animal cunning–'course I don't hold much with that, but some do. Some do. But there's some varmints that do damage and just plain got to be killed. Understand?"

"I . . . think so. But what about what you said about a man dying when he kills something?"

"Man kills once and he starts to get callous. Next time it ain't so hard. Then you get so's you make a decision that something's got to die and you kill it, just like that. Then you dead, boy. You got no feeling no more so you just as good as dead. You just ain't had time to lay down."

Tommy wiggled his toes and got no response. They felt like sticks of wood, stilts that somebody had glued on his legs. An ant left the ground and started climbing his arm until he blew, softly, blew the ant into some brave new world. The mist was thinning and the sun began to shine dully through the trees. Pa was right, he thought. Seems as if everything had a place in the scheme of things. Birds ate worms they found on the ground. Then they got eaten by bigger birds. Rabbits got eaten by foxes and foxes by bobcats, and bobcats by bears or something all the way up to elephants. And elephants were killed by man. Pa said that man preyed on himself, whatever that meant, but everything had a place, and when they got out of place they upset the balance. Like too many rabbits or squirrels or anything.

"After the horror of atheism, there is nothing that leads weak minds further astray from the paths of virtue than the idea that the minds of other animals resemble our own, and that, therefore, we have no greater right to future life than have gnats and ants."

René Descartes—"A Treatise on the Passions of the Soul"—1649

A twig snapped like dynamite and he froze on the ground and swiveled the gun to the left and waited. Slowly, clumsily, with three blades of grass waving like pennants ahead of him, a porcupine strolled into view, made his way through the sunlight, and vanished into the grass. Tommy laughed, out loud almost, he could hardly keep from blowing up he was so relieved, so happy. Instead he settled down again to wait.

But things had changed somehow. The sunlight was duller, almost disappearing and he felt a chill again as he had before the sun came up. And the silence somehow nettled him . . . *the silence!* Not a sound! No crickets, no chirping, no rustling, nothing. There was something out there! The happy-scared feeling ran up and down Tommy's back and his breath came in painful gasps. His chest hammered, almost pushing his lungs into his mouth with its rhythm which seemed to be saying: *Soon! Soon! Soon they would be calling him Tom Grimes like his father. Soon he would be able to go into the Hut and drink liquor with the rest of the men. Soon the waiting would be over. Soon he would be grown. Soon. Soon. Soon. Soon! Soon! Soon!*

"It's always the old who lead us to
the wars,
Always the young who fall.
Look at all we've won
With the sabre and the gun,
Now tell me, is it worth it all?
Call it peace or call it treason,
Call it love or call it reason,
But I ain't a-marching any more."

Phil Ochs

There! In the bushes! A little pinch of color behind the bramble bush moving light and easy, so very easy, behind the bushes. He slid down still further behind the gun and spread his feet wide, toes digging into the soft earth. "Put the whole side of your body behind the gun to take the recoil," Pa had said. "Spread your legs wide to brace yourself. Make the gun, your arm, your hip, your leg into one long line." Tommy drew his breath in and nearly gagged trying to hold it, sighting along the clean black ridges of the rifle. The outline was clear behind the bush, creeping, sniffling, gliding along.

"You won't see it, or hear it, or smell it, or anything," Pa had told him. "You'll just feel it, and it'll be there."

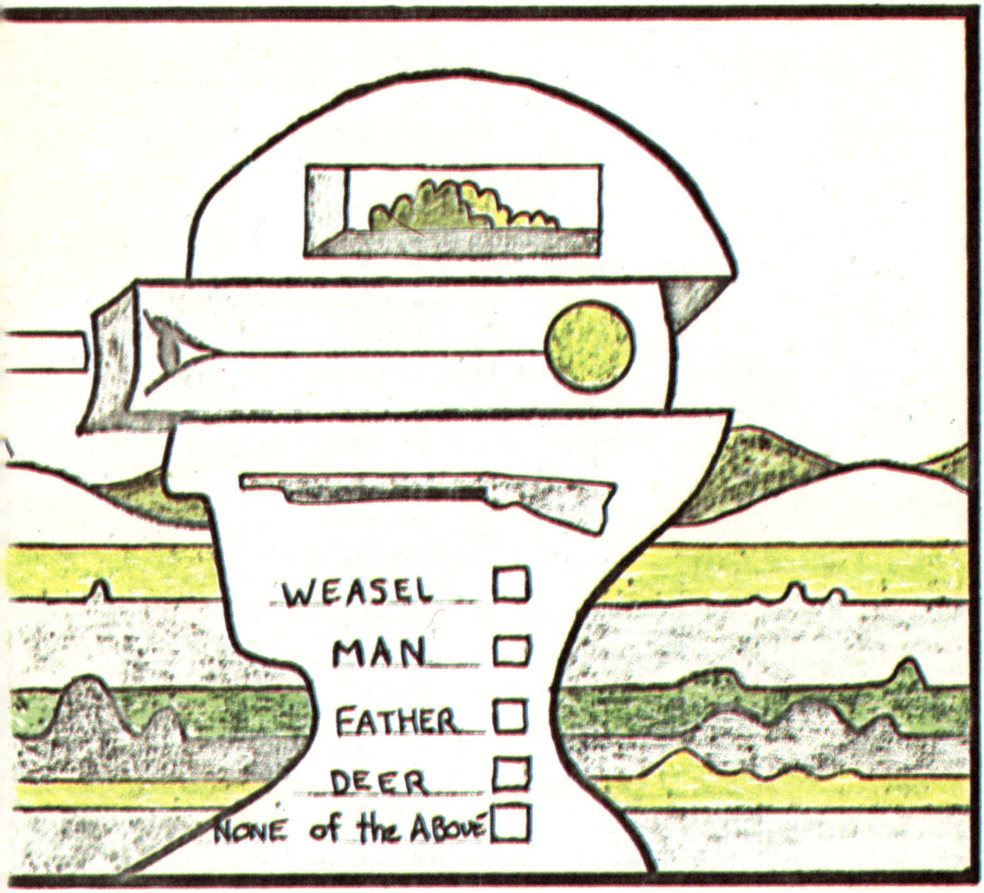

Tommy breathed out and in, let some of the air out and chokingly began to squeeze the trigger. Would it never go off, his mind asked, reeling and stumbling and clinging desperately to reality, and the earth stuttered. The light blinked. His ears rang. His nose reacted to the smell of smoke and the taste of ink crept into his mouth. There was a rustling sound in the bushes and a thrashing, a terrible thrashing and rattling, but it stopped. Suddenly it stopped. Tommy blinked. It was over; just like that, it was over.

He got to his feet and the stiffness forced him to lean against a tree trunk. Before there had been nothing, then suddenly there was something, a small patch of color the same as Pa's jacket. Tommy blinked and listened for the crashing sound of someone coming through the forest—but there was nothing. Nothing. He strained his ears and heard new-sprung crickets and birdcalls, but no crashing, no rustling, no voice, and he started for the bush and then stopped, trembling.

"Pa?" he whispered, "Pa-a-a?" There was no sound except his own voice, twisted and shapeless and mocking, twirling through the trees like vapors in the dull, chilly air. "Pa! Pa! Pa!"

Then came the rushing and the crashing to the left and the tall husky figure coming out of the gloom saying, "Boy? What's wrong, boy?" And Tommy ran over and slammed his head against his father's chest. "Pa! I thought I killed you, Pa, I thought I killed you, Pa, I thought I killed a man!"

"Now, Tommy, it's all right, everything's all right," Pa said, walking behind the bush and kneeling and then rising and coming back.

"See?" he said. "What did I tell you? Right through the heart. Now that's good shooting. Come over here and look; come on, now."

So he looked, and then it wasn't so bad.

Later, much later, they walked the mile from town to the Hut and walked inside together. There were some men sitting at tables and they looked up as Pa hoisted him onto the bar, running his fingers through his dark, blond hair.

"Boys, I wanna tell you my boy became a man today. Yessir, killed his first nigger."

Yessir, killed his first nigger.

Yessir, killed his first nigger.

Yessir, killed his first nigger.

Yessir, killed his first nigger.

Yessir, killed his first nigger.

Yessir, killed his first nigger.

Yessir, killed his first nigger.

Yessir, killed his first nigger.

Yessir, killed his first nigger.

"No!" a man said. "Who?"

"Swamp-buck got away from the chain gang yes-tidy."

"Git out!" the man said.

"Yessir, got him right through the heart."

The man grabbed Tommy and hugged him around the knees. "You a man now, boy!" he yelled, "you a real live honest-to-goodness 'fore God man!"

And Pa, his blue eyes agleam, yelled out, "Bartender! Don't just stand there! Give this man a drink!"

The man sat Tommy down on the bar and the liquor made him cough a bit as it coursed down his throat and it made his ears ring like the tolling of bells. But he smiled happily as the feeling of warmth like Mississippi sunshine spread through his insides. For now he belonged.

The bell doth toll for him that thinks it doth. No man is an island, entire of itself; every man is a piece of the continent, a part of the main. Any man's death diminishes me because I am involved in mankind, and therefore never send to know for whom the bell tolls; it tolls for thee.

John Donne, *Meditation XVII,* 1623-1624

The Celestial Omnibus

E.M.Forster

The boy who resided at Agathox Lodge, 28, Buckingham Park Road, Surbiton, had often been puzzled by the old sign-post that stood almost opposite. He asked his mother about it, and she replied that it was a joke, and not a very nice one, which had been made many years back by some naughty young men, and that the police ought to remove it. For there were two strange things about this sign-post: firstly, it pointed up a blank alley, and, secondly, it had painted on it, in faded characters, the words, "To Heaven."

"What kind of young men were they?" he asked.

"I think your father told me that one of them wrote verses, and was expelled from the University and came to grief in other ways. Still, it was a long time ago. You must ask your father about it. He will say the same as I do, that it was put up as a joke."

"So it doesn't mean anything at all?"

She sent him up-stairs to put on his best things, for the Bonses were coming to tea, and he was to hand the cake-stand.

It struck him, as he wrenched on his tightening trousers, that he might do worse than ask Mr. Bons about the sign-post. His father, though very kind, always laughed at him—shrieked with laughter whenever he or any other child asked a question or spoke. But Mr. Bons was serious as well as kind. He had a beautiful house and lent one books, he was a churchwarden, and a candidate for the County Council; he had donated to the Free Library enormously, he presided over the Literary Society, and had Members of Parliament to stop with him—in short, he was probably the wisest person alive.

Yet even Mr. Bons could only say that the sign-post was a joke—the joke of a person named Shelley.

"Of course!" cried the mother; "I told you so, dear. That was the name."

"Had you never heard of Shelley?" asked Mr. Bons.

"No," said the boy, and hung his head.

"But is there no Shelley in the house?"

Mr. Bons must be the wisest person

"Why, yes!" exclaimed the lady, in much agitation. "Dear Mr. Bons, we aren't such Philistines as that. Two at the least. One a wedding present, and the other, smaller print, in one of the spare rooms."

"I believe we have seven Shelleys," said Mr. Bons, with a slow smile. Then he brushed the cake crumbs off his stomach, and, together with his daughter, rose to go.

The boy, obeying a wink from his mother, saw them all the way to the garden gate, and when they had gone he did not at once return to the house, but gazed for a little up and down Buckingham Park Road.

His parents lived at the right end of it. After No. 39 the quality of the houses dropped very suddenly, and 64 had not even a separate servants' entrance. But at the present moment the whole road looked rather pretty, for the sun had just set in splendour, and the inequalities of rent were drowned in a saffron afterglow. Small birds twittered, and the breadwinners' train shrieked musically down through the cutting—that wonderful cutting which has drawn to itself the whole beauty out of Surbiton, and clad itself, like any Alpine valley, with the glory of the fir and the silver birch and the primrose. It was this cutting that had first stirred desires within the boy—desires for something just a little different, he knew not what, desires that would return whenever things were sunlit, as they were this evening, running up and down inside him, up and down, up and down, till he would feel quite unusual all over, and as likely as not would want to cry. This evening he was even sillier, for he slipped across the road towards the sign-post and began to run up the blank alley.

The alley runs between high walls—the walls of the gardens of "Ivanhoe" and "Belle Vista" respectively. It smells a little all the way, and is scarcely twenty yards long, including the turn at the end. So not unnaturally the boy soon came to a standstill. "I'd like to kick that Shelley," he exclaimed, and glanced idly at a piece of paper which was pasted on the wall. Rather an odd piece of paper, and he read it carefully before he turned back. This is what he read:

alive. He owns seven Shelleys.

S. and C. R. C. C.

Alteration in Service.

Owing to lack of patronage the Company are regretfully compelled to suspend the hourly service, and to retain only the

Sunrise and Sunset Omnibuses,

which will run as usual. It is to be hoped that the public will patronize an arrangement which is intended for their convenience. As an extra inducement, the Company will, for the first time, now issue

Return Tickets!

(available one day only), which may be obtained of the driver. Passengers are again reminded that *no tickets are issued at the other end*, and that no complaints in this connection will receive consideration from the Company. Nor will the Company be responsible for any negligence or stupidity on the part of Passengers, nor for Hailstorms, Lightning, Loss of Tickets, nor for any Act of God.

For the Direction.

Now he had never seen this notice before, nor could he imagine where the omnibus went to. S. of course was for Surbiton, and R.C.C. meant Road Car Company. But what was the meaning of the other C.? Coombe and Malden, perhaps, or possibly "City." Yet it could not hope to compete with the South-Western. The whole thing, the boy reflected, was run on hopelessly unbusiness-like lines. Why no tickets from the other end? And what an hour to start! Then he realized that unless the notice was a hoax, an omnibus must have been starting just as he was wishing the Bonses goodbye. He peered at the ground through the gathering dusk, and there he saw what might or might not be the marks of wheels. Yet nothing had come out of the alley. And he had never seen an omnibus at any time in the Buckingham Park Road. No: it must be a hoax, like the sign-posts, like the fairy tales, like the dreams upon which he would wake suddenly in the night. And with a sigh he stepped from the alley—right into the arms of his father.

Oh, how his father laughed! "Poor, poor Popsey!" he cried, "Diddums! Diddums! Diddums think he'd walky-palky up to Evvink!" And his mother, also convulsed with laughter, appeared on the steps of Agathox Lodge. "Don't Bob!" she gasped. "Don't be so naughty! Oh, you'll kill me! Oh, leave the boy alone!"

But all the evening the joke was kept up. The father implored to be taken too. Was it a very tiring walk? Need one wipe one's shoes on the door-mat? And the boy went to bed feeling faint and sore, and thankful for only one thing—that he had not said a word about the omnibus. It was a hoax, yet through his dreams it grew more and more real, and the streets of Surbiton, through which he saw it driving, seemed instead to become hoaxes and shadows. And very early in the morning he woke with a cry, for he had had a glimpse of its destination.

He struck a match, and its light fell not only on his watch but also on his calendar, so that he knew it to be half-an-hour to sunrise. It was pitch dark, for the fog had come down from London in the night, and all Surbiton was wrapped in its embraces. Yet he sprang out and dressed himself, for he was determined to settle once for all which was real: the omnibus or the streets. "I shall be a fool one way or the other," he thought, "until I know." Soon he was shivering in the road under the gas lamp that guarded the entrance to the alley.

To enter the alley itself required some courage. Not only was it horribly dark, but he now realized that it was an impossible terminus for an omnibus. If it had not been for a policeman, whom he heard approaching through the fog, he would never have made the attempt. The next moment he had made the attempt and failed. Nothing. Nothing but a blank alley and a very silly boy gaping at its dirty floor. It *was* a hoax. "I'll tell papa and mamma," he decided. "I deserve it. I deserve that they should know. I am too silly to be alive." And he went back to the gate of Agathox Lodge.

There he remembered that his watch was fast. The sun was not risen; it would not rise for two minutes. "Give the bus every chance," he thought cynically, and returned into the alley.

But the omnibus was there.

II

It had two horses, whose sides were still smoking from their journey, and its two great lamps shone through the fog against the alley's walls, changing their cobwebs and moss into tissues of fairyland. The driver was huddled up in a cape. He faced the blank wall, and how he had managed to drive in so neatly and so silently was one of the many things that the boy never discovered. Nor could he imagine how ever he would drive out.

"Please," his voice quavered through the foul brown air, "Please, is that an omnibus?"

"Omnibus est," said the driver, without turning round. There was a moment's silence. The policeman passed, coughing, by the entrance of the alley. The boy crouched in the shadow, for he did not want to be found out. He was pretty sure, too, that it was a Pirate; nothing else, he reasoned, would go from such odd places and at such odd hours.

"About when do you start?" He tried to sound nonchalant.

"At sunrise."

"How far do you go?"

"The whole way."

"And can I have a return ticket which will bring me all the way back?"

"You can."

"Do you know, I half think I'll come." The driver made no answer. The sun must have risen, for he unhitched the brake. And scarcely had the boy jumped in before the omnibus was off.

How? Did it turn? There was no room. Did it go forward? There was a blank wall. Yet it was moving—moving at a stately pace through the fog, which had turned from brown to yellow. The thought of warm bed and warmer breakfast made the boy feel faint. He wished he had not come. His parents would not have approved. He would have gone back to them if the weather had not made it impossible. The solitude was terrible; he was the only passenger. And the omnibus, though wellbuilt, was cold and somewhat musty. He drew his coat round him, and in so doing chanced to feel his pocket. It was empty. He had forgotten his purse.

"Stop!" he shouted. "Stop!" And then, being of a polite disposition, he glanced up at the painted notice-board so that he might call the driver by name. "Mr. Browne! stop; O, do please stop!"

Mr. Browne did not stop, but he opened a little window and looked in at the boy. His face was a surprise, so kind it was and modest.

"Mr. Browne, I've left my purse behind. I've not got a penny. I can't pay for the ticket. Will you take my watch, please? I am in the most awful hole."

"Tickets on this line," said the driver, "whether single or return, can be purchased by coinage from no terrene mint. And a chronometer, though it had solaced the vigils of Charlemagne, or measured the slumbers of Laura, can acquire by no mutation the double-cake that charms the fangless Cerberus of Heaven!" So saying, he handed in the necessary ticket, and, while the boy said "Thank you," continued: "Titular pretcnsions, I know it wcll, arc vanity. Yet they merit no censure when uttered on a laughing lip, and in an homonymous world are in some sort useful, since they do serve to distinguish one Jack from his fellow. Remember me, therefore, as Sir Thomas Browne."

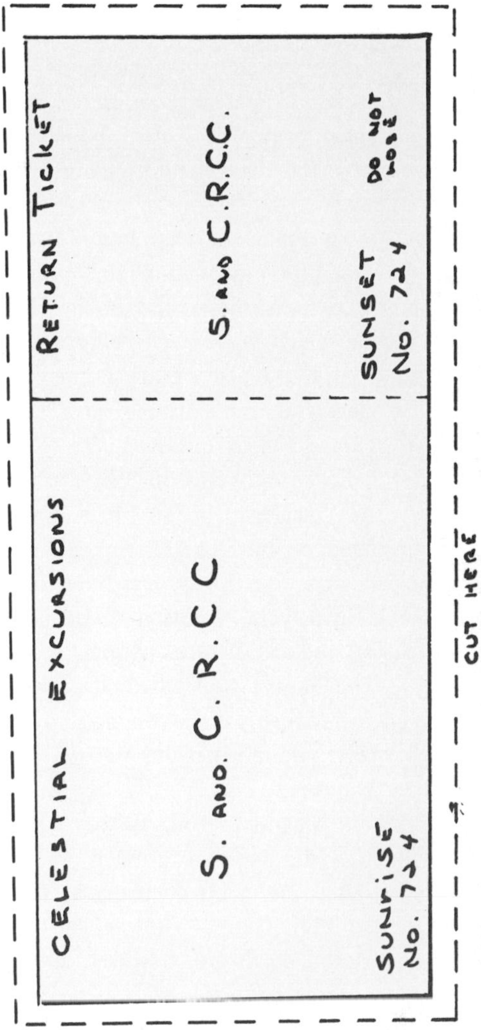

"Are you a Sir? Oh, sorry!" He had heard of these gentlemen drivers. "It *is* good of you about the ticket. But if you go on at this rate, however does your bus pay?"

"It does not pay. It was not intended to pay. Many are the faults of my equipage; it is compounded too curiously of foreign woods; its cushions tickle erudition rather than promote repose; and my horses are nourished not on the evergreen pastures of the moment, but on the dried bents and clovers of Latinity. But that it pays!—that error at all events was never intended and never attained."

"Sorry again," said the boy rather hopelessly. Sir Thomas looked sad, fearing that, even for a moment, he had been the cause of sadness. He invited the boy to come up and sit beside him on the box, and together they journeyed on through the fog, which was now changing from yellow to white. There were no houses by the road; so it must be either Putney Heath or Wimbledon Common.

"Have you been a driver always?"

"I was a physician once."

"But why did you stop? Weren't you good?"

"As a healer of bodies I had scant success, and several score of my patients preceded me. But as a healer of the spirit I have succeeded beyond my hopes and my deserts. For though my draughts were not better nor subtler than those of other men, yet, by reason of the cunning goblets wherein I offered them, the queasy soul was ofttimes tempted to sip and be refreshed."

"The queasy soul," he murmured; "if the sun sets with trees in front of it, and you suddenly come strange all over, is that a queasy soul?"

"Have you felt that?"

"Why yes."

After a pause he told the boy a little, a very little, about the journey's end. But they did not chatter much, for the boy, when he liked a person, would as soon sit silent in his company as speak, and this, he discovered, was also the mind of Sir Thomas Browne and of many others with whom he was to be acquainted. He heard, however, about the young man Shelley, who was now quite a famous person, with a carriage of his own, and about some of the other drivers who are in the service of the Company. Meanwhile the light grew stronger, though the fog did not disperse. It was now more like mist than fog, and at times would travel quickly across them, as if it was part of a cloud. They had been ascending, too, in a most puzzling way; for over two hours the horses had been pulling against the collar, and even if it were Richmond Hill they ought to have been at the top long ago. Perhaps it was Epsom, or even the North Downs; yet the air seemed keener than that which blows on either. And as to the name of their destination, Sir Thomas Browne was silent.

Crash!

"Thunder, by Jove!" said the boy, "and not so far off either. Listen to the echoes! It's more like mountains."

He thought, not very vividly, of his father and mother. He saw them sitting down to sausages and listening to the storm. He saw his own empty place. Then there would be questions, alarms, theories, jokes, consolations. They would expect him back at lunch. To lunch he would not come, nor to tea, but he would be in for dinner, and so his day's truancy would be over. If he had had his purse he would have bought them presents–not that he should have known what to get them.

Crash!

The peal and the lightning came together. The cloud quivered as if it were alive, and torn streamers of mist rushed past. "Are you afraid?" asked Sir Thomas Browne.

"What is there to be afraid of? Is it much farther?"

The horses of the omnibus stopped just as a ball of fire burst up and exploded with a ringing noise that was deafening but clear, like the noise of a blacksmith's forge. All the cloud was shattered.

"Oh, listen, Sir Thomas Browne! No, I mean look; we shall get a view at last. No. I mean listen; that sounds like a rainbow!"

The noise had died into the faintest murmur, beneath which another murmur grew, spreading stealthily, steadily, in a curve that widened but did not vary. And in widening curves a rainbow was spreading from the horses' feet into the dissolving mists.

"But how beautiful! What colours! Where will it stop? It is more like the rainbows you can tread on. More like dreams."

The colour and the sound grew together. The rainbow spanned an enormous gulf. Clouds rushed under it and were pierced by it, and still it grew, reaching forward, conquering the darkness, until it touched something that seemed more solid than a cloud.

The boy stood up. "What is that out there?" he called. "What does it rest on, out at that other end?"

In the morning sunshine a precipice shone forth beyond the gulf. A precipice–or was it a castle? The horses moved. They set their feet upon the rainbow.

"Oh, look!" the boy shouted. "Oh, listen! Those caves–or are they gateways? Oh, look between those cliffs at those ledges. I see people! I see trees!"

"Look also below," whispered Sir Thomas. "Neglect not the diviner Acheron."

The boy looked below, past the flames of the rainbow that licked against their wheels. The gulf also had cleared, and in its depths there flowed an everlasting river. One sunbeam entered and struck a green pool, and as they passed over he saw three maidens rise to the surface of the pool, singing, and playing with something that glistened like a ring.

"You down in the water–" he called.

They answered, "You up on the bridge–" There was a burst of music. "You up on the bridge, good luck to you. Truth in the depth, truth on the height."

"You down in the water, what are you doing?"

Sir Thomas Browne replied: "They sport in the mancipiary possession of their gold"; and the omnibus arrived.

III

The boy was in disgrace. He sat locked up in the nursery of Agathox Lodge, learning poetry for a punishment. His father had said, "My boy! I can pardon anything but untruthfulness," and had caned him, saying at each stroke, "There is *no* omnibus, *no* driver, *no* bridge, *no* mountain; you are a *truant*, a *gutter snipe*, a *liar*." His father could be very stern at times. His mother had begged him to say he was sorry. But he could not say that. It was the greatest day of his life, in spite of the caning and the poetry at the end of it.

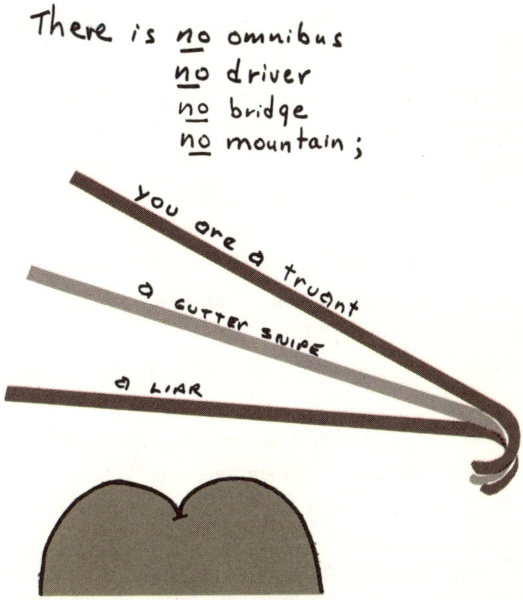

He had returned punctually at sunset—driven not by Sir Thomas Browne, but by a maiden lady who was full of quiet fun. They had talked of omnibuses and also of barouche landaus. How far away her gentle voice seemed now! Yet it was scarcely three hours since he had left her up the alley.

His mother called through the door. "Dear, you are to come down and to bring your poetry with you."

He came down and found that Mr. Bons was in the smoking-room with his father. It had been a dinner party.

"Here is the great traveller!" said his father grimly. "Here is the young gentleman who drives in an omnibus over rainbows, while young ladies sing to him." Pleased with his wit, he laughed.

"After all," said Mr. Bons, smiling, "there is something a little like it in Wagner. It is odd how, in quite illiterate minds, you will find glimmers of Artistic Truth. The case interests me. Let me plead for the culprit. We have all romanced in our time, haven't we?"

"Hear how kind Mr. Bons is," said his mother, while his father said, "Very well. Let him say his Poem, and that will do. He is going away to my sister on Tuesday, and *she* will cure him of this alley-slopering." (Laughter.) "Say your Poem."

The boy began, " 'Standing aloof in giant ignorance.' "

His father laughed again–roared. "One for you, my son! 'Standing aloof in giant ignorance!' I never knew these poets talked sense. Just describes you. Here, Bons, you go in for poetry. Put him through it, will you, while I fetch up the whisky?"

"Yes, give me the Keats," said Mr. Bons. "Let him say his Keats to me."

So for a few moments the wise man and the ignorant boy were left alone in the smoking-room.

" 'Standing aloof in giant ignorance, of thee I dream and of the Cyclades, as one who sits ashore and longs perchance to visit–' "

"Quite right. To visit what?"

" 'To visit dolphin coral in deep seas,' " said the boy, and burst into tears.

"Come, come! why do you cry?"

"Because–because all these words that only rhymed before, now that I've come back they're me."

Mr. Bons laid the Keats down. The case was more interesting than he had expected. "*You?*" he exclaimed. "This sonnet, *you*?"

"Yes–and look further on: 'Aye, on the shores of darkness there is light, and precipices show untrodden green.' It *is* so, sir. All these things are true."

"I never doubted it," said Mr. Bons, with closed eyes.

"You–then you believe me? You believe in the omnibus and the driver and the storm and that return ticket I got for nothing and–"

"Tut, tut! No more of your yarns, my boy. I meant that I never doubted the essential truth of Poetry. Some day, when you have read more, you will understand what I mean."

"But Mr. Bons, it *is* so. There *is* light upon the shores of darkness. I have seen it coming. Light and a wind."

"Nonsense," said Mr. Bons.

"If I had stopped! They tempted me. They told me to give up my ticket—for you cannot come back if you lose your ticket. They called from the river for it, and indeed I was tempted, for I have never been so happy as among those precipices. But I thought of my mother and father, and that I must fetch them. Yet they will not come, though the road starts opposite our house. It has all happened as the people up there warned me, and Mr. Bons has disbelieved me like every one else. I have been caned. I shall never see that mountain again."

"What's that about me?" said Mr. Bons, sitting up in his chair very suddenly.

"I told them about you, and how clever you were, and how many books you had, and they said, 'Mr. Bons will certainly disbelieve you.' "

"Stuff and nonsense, my young friend. You grow impertinent. I—well—I will settle the matter. Not a word to your father. I will cure you. Tomorrow evening I will myself call here to take you for a walk, and at sunset we will go up this alley opposite and hunt for your omnibus, you silly little boy."

His face grew serious, for the boy was not disconcerted, but leapt about the room singing, "Joy! joy! I told them you would believe me. We will drive together over the rainbow. I told them that you would come." After all, could there be anything in the story? Wagner? Keats? Shelley? Sir Thomas Browne? Certainly the case was interesting.

And on the morrow evening, though it was pouring with rain, Mr. Bons did not omit to call at Agathox Lodge.

The boy was ready, bubbling with excitement, and skipping about in a way that rather vexed the President of the Literary Society. They took a turn down Buckingham Park Road, and then—having seen that no one was watching them—slipped up the alley. Naturally enough (for the sun was setting) they ran straight against the omnibus.

"Good heavens!" exclaimed Mr. Bons. "Good gracious heavens!"

It was not the omnibus in which the boy had driven first, nor yet that in which he had returned. There were three horses—black, gray, and white, the gray being the finest. The driver, who turned round at the mention of goodness and of heaven, was a sallow man with terrifying jaws and sunken eyes. Mr. Bons, on seeing him, gave a cry as if of recognition, and began to tremble violently.

The boy jumped in.

"Is it possible?" cried Mr. Bons. "Is the impossible possible?"

"Sir; come in, sir. It is such a fine omnibus. Oh, here is his name—Dan some one."

Lasciate Ogni Baldanza Voi Che Entrate *

Mr. Bons sprang in too. A blast of wind immediately slammed the omnibus door, and the shock jerked down all the omnibus blinds, which were very weak on their springs.

"Dan . . . Show me. Good gracious heavens! we're moving."

"Hooray!" said the boy.

Mr. Bons became flustered. He had not intended to be kidnapped. He could not find the doorhandle, nor push up the blinds. The omnibus was quite dark, and by the time he had struck a match, night had come on outside also. They were moving rapidly.

"A strange, a memorable adventure," he said, surveying the interior of the omnibus, which was large, roomy, and constructed with extreme regularity, every part exactly answering to every other part. Over the door (the handle of which was outside) was written, "Lasciate ogni baldanza voi che entrate"—at least, that was what was written, but Mr. Bons said that it was Lashy arty something, and that baldanza was a mistake for speranza. His voice sounded as if he was in church. Meanwhile, the boy called to the cadaverous driver for two return tickets. They were handed in without a word. Mr. Bons covered his face with his hands and again trembled. "Do you know who that is!" he whispered, when the little window had shut upon them. "It is the impossible."

"Well, I don't like him as much as Sir Thomas Browne, though I shouldn't be surprised if he had even more in him."

"More in him?" He stamped irritably. "By accident you have made the greatest discovery of the century, and all you can say is that there is more in this man. Do you remember those vellum books in my library, stamped with red lilies? This—sit still, I bring you stupendous news!—*this is the man who wrote them*."

Abandon all despair ye who enter here
baldanza = despair; speranza = hope

"the man who wrote my vellum books!"

The boy sat quite still. "I wonder if we shall see Mrs. Gamp?" he asked, after a civil pause.

"Mrs.–?"

"Mrs. Gamp and Mrs. Harris. I like Mrs. Harris. I came upon them quite suddenly. Mrs. Gamp's bandboxes have moved over the rainbow so badly. All the bottoms have fallen out, and two of the pippins off her bedstead tumbled into the stream."

"Out there sits the man who wrote my vellum books!" thundered Mr. Bons, "and you talk to me of Dickens and of Mrs. Gamp?"

"I know Mrs. Gamp so well," he apologized. "I could not help being glad to see her. I recognized her voice. She was telling Mrs. Harris about Mrs. Prig."

"Did you spend the whole day in her elevating company?"

"Oh, no. I raced. I met a man who took me out beyond to a race-course. You run, and there are dolphins out at sea."

"Indeed. Do you remember the man's name?"

"Achilles. No; he was later. Tom Jones."

Mr. Bons sighed heavily. "Well, my lad, you have made a miserable mess of it. Think of a cultured person with your opportunities! A cultured person would have known all these characters and known what to have said to each. He would not have wasted his time with a Mrs. Gamp or a Tom Jones. The creations of Homer, of Shakespeare, and of Him who drives us now, would alone have contented him. He would not have raced. He would have asked intelligent questions."

"But Mr. Bons," said the boy humbly, "you will be a cultured person. I told them so."

"True, true, and I beg of you not to disgrace me when we arrive. No gossiping. No running. Keep close to my side, and never speak to these Immortals unless they speak to you. Yes, and give me the return tickets. You will be losing them."

The boy surrendered the tickets, but felt a little sore. After all, he had found the way to this place. It was hard first to be disbelieved and then to be lectured. Meanwhile, the rain had stopped, and moonlight crept into the omnibus through the cracks in the blinds.

"But how is there to be a rainbow?" cried the boy.

"You distract me," snapped Mr. Bons. "I wish to meditate on beauty. I wish to goodness I was with a reverent and sympathetic person."

The lad bit his lip. He made a hundred good resolutions. He would imitate Mr. Bons all the visit. He would not laugh, or run, or sing, or do any of the vulgar things that must have disgusted his new friends last time. He would be very careful to pronounce their names properly, and to remember who knew whom.

After all, he had found the way to this place.

Achilles did not know Tom Jones—at least, so Mr. Bons said. The Duchess of Malfi was older than Mrs. Gamp—at least, so Mr. Bons said. He would be self-conscious, reticent, and prim. He would never say he liked any one. Yet, when the blind flew up at a chance touch of his head, all these good resolutions went to the winds, for the omnibus had reached the summit of a moonlit hill, and there was the chasm, and there, across it, stood the old precipices, dreaming, with their feet in the everlasting river. He exclaimed, "The mountain! Listen to the new tune in the water! Look at the camp fires in the ravines," and Mr. Bons, after a hasty glance, retorted, "Water? Camp fires? Ridiculous rubbish. Hold your tongue. There is nothing at all."

Yet, under his eyes, a rainbow formed, compounded not of sunlight and storm, but of moonlight and the spray of the river. The three horses put their feet upon it. He thought it the finest rainbow he had seen, but did not dare to say so, since Mr. Bons said that nothing was there. He leant out—the window had opened—and sang the tune that rose from the sleeping waters.

"The prelude to Rhinegold?" said Mr. Bons suddenly. "Who taught you these *leit motifs*?" He, too, looked out of the window. Then he behaved very oddly. He gave a choking cry, and fell back on to the omnibus floor He writhed and kicked. His face was green.

"Does the bridge make you dizzy?" the boy asked.

"Dizzy!" gasped Mr. Bons. "I want to go back. Tell the driver."

But the driver shook his head.

"We are nearly there," said the boy. "They are asleep. Shall I call? They will be so pleased to see you, for I have prepared them."

Mr. Bons moaned. They moved over the lunar rainbow, which ever and ever broke away behind their wheels. How still the night was! Who would be sentry at the Gate?

"I am coming," he shouted, again forgetting the hundred resolutions. "I am returning—I, the boy."

"The boy is returning," cried a voice to other voices, who repeated, "The boy is returning."

"I am bringing Mr. Bons with me."

Silence.

"I should have said Mr. Bons is bringing me with him."

Profound silence.

"Who stands sentry?"

"Achilles."

And on the rocky causeway, close to the springing of the rainbow bridge, he saw a young man who carried a wonderful shield.

"Mr. Bons, it is Achilles, armed."

"I want to go back," said Mr. Bons.

The last fragment of the rainbow melted, the wheels sang upon the living rock, the door of the omnibus burst open. Out leapt the boy—he could not resist—and sprang to meet the warrior, who, stooping suddenly, caught him on his shield.

"Achilles!" he cried, "let me get down, for I am ignorant and vulgar, and I must wait for that Mr. Bons of whom I told you yesterday."

But Achilles raised him aloft. He crouched on the wonderful shield, on heroes and burning cities, on vineyards graven in gold, on every dear passion, every joy, on the entire image of the Mountain that he had discovered, encircled, like it, with an everlasting stream. "No, no," he protested, "I am not worthy. It is Mr. Bons who must be up here."

But Mr. Bons was whimpering, and Achilles trumpeted and cried, "Stand upright upon my shield!"

"Sir, I did not mean to stand! Something made me stand. Sir, why do you delay? Here is only the great Achillēs, whom you knew."

Mr. Bons screamed, "I see no one. I see nothing. I want to go back."

stirred desires within the boy - desires for something just a little different.

Then he cried to the driver, "Save me! Let me stop in your chariot. I have honoured you. I have quoted you. I have bound you in vellum. Take me back to my world."

The driver replied, "I am the means and not the end. I am the food and not the life. Stand by yourself, as that boy has stood. I cannot save you. For poetry is a spirit; and they that would worship it must worship in spirit and in truth."

Mr. Bons–he could not resist–crawled out of the beautiful omnibus. His face appeared, gaping horribly. His hands followed, one gripping the step, the other beating the air. Now his shoulders emerged, his chest, his stomach. With a shriek of "I see London," he fell–fell against the hard, moonlit rock, fell into it as if it were water, fell through it, vanished, and was seen by the boy no more.

"Where have you fallen to, Mr. Bons? Here is a procession arriving to honour you with music and torches. Here come the men and women whose names you know. The mountain is awake, the river is awake, over the race-course the sea is awaking those dolphins, and it is all for you. They want you——"

There was the touch of fresh leaves on his forehead. Some one had crowned him.

ΤΕΛΟΣ

From the *Kingston Gazette, Surbiton Times,* and *Raynes Park Observer.*

The body of Mr. Septimus Bons has been found in a shockingly mutilated condition in the vicinity of the Bermondsey gas-works. The deceased's pockets contained a sovereign-purse, a silver cigar-case, a bijou pronouncing dictionary, and a couple of omnibus tickets. The unfortunate gentleman had apparently been hurled from a considerable height. Foul play is suspected, and a thorough investigation is pending by the authorities.

Frame-Tale

John Barth

Cut on dotted line.
Twist end once and fasten
AB to *ab*, *CD* to *cd*.

A *B*

ONCE UPON A TIME THERE

D *C*

(continued)

WAS A STORY THAT BEGAN

(continued)

A Couple of Hamburgers

James Thurber

It had been raining for a long time, a slow, cold rain falling out of iron-colored clouds. They had been driving since morning and they still had a hundred and thirty miles to go. It was about three o'clock in the afternoon. "I'm getting hungry," she said. He took his eyes off the wet, winding road for a fraction of a second and said, "We'll stop at a dog-wagon." She shifted her position irritably. "I wish you wouldn't call them *dog*-wagons," she said. He pressed the klaxon button and went around a slow car. "That's what they are," he said. "Dog-wagons." She waited a few seconds. *"Decent* people call them *diners,"* she told him, and added, "Even if you call them diners, I don't like them." He speeded up a hill. "They have better stuff than most restaurants," he said. "Anyway, I want to get home before dark and it takes too long in a restaurant. We can stay our stomachs with a couple hamburgers." She lighted a cigarette and he asked her to light one for him. She lighted one deliberately and handed it to him. "I wish you wouldn't say 'stay our stomachs,' " she said. "You know I hate that. It's like 'sticking to your ribs.' You say that all the time." He grinned. "Good old American expressions, both of them," he said. "Like sow belly. Old pioneer term, sow belly." She sniffed. "My ancestors were pioneers, too. You don't have to be vulgar just because you were a pioneer." "Your ancestors never got as far west as mine did," he said. "The real pioneers travelled on their sow belly and got somewhere." He laughed loudly at that. She looked out at the wet trees and signs and telephone poles going by. They drove on for several miles without a word; he kept chortling every now and then.

"What's that funny sound?" she asked, suddenly. It invariably made him angry when she heard a funny sound. "What funny sound?" he demanded. "You're always hearing funny sounds." She laughed briefly. "That's what you said when the bearing burned out," she reminded him. "You'd never have noticed it if it hadn't been for me." "I noticed it, all right," he said. "Yes," she said. "When it was too late." She enjoyed bringing up the subject of the burned-out bearing whenever he got to chortling. "It was too late when *you* noticed it, as far as that goes," he said. Then, after a pause, "Well, what does it sound like *this* time? All engines make a noise running, you know." "I know all about that," she answered. "It sounds like–it sounds like a lot of safety pins being jiggled around in a tumbler." He snorted. "That's your imagination. Nothing gets the matter with a car that sounds like a lot of safety pins. I happen to know that." She tossed away her cigarette. "Oh, sure," she said. "You always happen to know everything." They drove on in silence.

"I want to stop somewhere and get something to *eat*!" she said loudly. "All right, all right!" he said. "I been watching for a dog-wagon, haven't I? There hasn't been any. I can't make you a dog-wagon." The wind blew rain in on her and she put up the window on her side all the way. "I won't stop at just any old diner," she said. "I won't stop unless it's a cute one." He looked around at her. "Unless it's a *what* one?" he shouted. "You know what I mean," she said. "I mean a decent, clean one where they don't slosh things at you. I hate to have a lot of milky coffee sloshed at me." "All right," he said. "We'll find a cute one, then. You pick it out. I wouldn't know. I might find one that was cunning but not cute." That struck him as funny and he began to chortle again. "Oh, shut up," she said.

Five miles farther along they came to a place called Sam's Diner. "Here's one," he said, slowing down. She looked it over. "I don't want to stop there," she said. "I don't like the ones that have nicknames." He brought the car to a stop at one side of the road. "Just what's the matter with the ones that have nicknames?" he asked with edgy, mock interest. "They're always Greek ones," she told him. "They're always Greek ones," he repeated after her. He set his teeth firmly together and started up again. After a time, "Good old Sam, the Greek," he said, in a singsong. "Good old Connecticut Sam Beardsley, the Greek." "You didn't see his name," she snapped. "Winthrop, then," he said. "Old Samuel Cabot Winthrop, the Greek dog-wagon man." He was getting hungry.

On the outskirts of the next town she said, as he slowed down, "It looks like a factory kind of town." He knew that she meant she wouldn't stop there. He drove on through the place. She lighted a cigarette as they pulled out into the open again. He slowed down and lighted a cigarette for himself. "Factory kind of town than *I* am!" he snarled. It was ten miles before they came to another town. "Torrington," he growled. "Happen to know there's a dog-wagon here because I stopped in it once with Bob Combs. Damn cute place, too, if you ask me." "I'm not asking you anything," she said, coldly. "You think you're *so* funny. I think I know the one you mean," she said, after a moment. "It's right in the town and it sits at an angle from the road. They're never so good, for some reason." He glared at her and almost ran up against the curb. "What the hell do you mean 'sits at an angle from the road'?" he cried. He was very hungry now. "Well, it isn't silly," she said, calmly. "I've noticed the ones that sit at an angle. They're cheaper, because they fitted them into funny little pieces of ground. The big ones parallel to the road are the best." He drove right through Torrington, his lips compressed. "Angle from the road, for God's sake!" he snarled, finally. She was looking out her window.

On the outskirts of the next town there was a diner called The Elite Diner. "This looks–" she began. "I see it, I see it!" he said. "It doesn't happen to look any cuter to me than any goddam–" She cut him off. "Don't be such a sorehead, for Lord's sake," she said. He pulled up and stopped beside the diner, and turned on her. "Listen," he said, grittingly, "I'm going to put down a couple of hamburgers in this place even if there isn't one single inch of chintz or cretonne in the whole–" "Oh, be still," she said. "You're just hungry and mean like a child. Eat your old hamburgers, what do I care?" Inside the place they sat down on stools and the counterman walked over to them, wiping up the counter top with a cloth as he did so. "What'll it be, folks?" he said. "Bad day, ain't it? Except for ducks." "I'll have a couple of–" began the husband, but his wife cut in. "I just want a pack of cigarettes," she said. He turned around slowly on his stool and stared at her as she put a dime and a nickel in the cigarette machine and ejected a package of Lucky Strikes. He turned to the counterman again. "I want a couple of hamburgers," he said. "With mustard and lots of onion. *Lots* of onion!" She hated onions. "I'll wait for you in the car," she said. He didn't answer and she went out.

He finished his hamburgers and his coffee slowly. It was terrible coffee. Then he went out to the car and got in and drove off, slowly humming "Who's Afraid of the Big Bad Wolf?" After a mile or so, "Well," he said, "what was the matter with the Elite Diner, milady?" "Didn't you *see* that cloth the man was wiping the counter with?" she demanded. "Ugh!" She shuddered. "I didn't happen to want to eat any of the counter," he said. He laughed at the comeback. "You didn't even notice it," she said. "You never notice anything. It was filthy." "I noticed they had some damn fine coffee in there," he said. "It was swell." He knew she loved good coffee. He began to hum his tune again; then he whistled it; then he began to sing it. She did not show her annoyance, but she knew that he knew she was annoyed. "Will you be kind enough to tell me what time it is?" she asked. "Big *bad* wolf, big *bad* wolf–five minutes o'five–tum-dee-*doo*-dee-dum-m-m." She settled back in her seat and took a cigarette from her case and tapped it on the case. "I'll wait till we get home," she said. "If you'll be kind enough to speed up a little." He drove on at the same speed. After a time he gave up the "Big Bad Wolf" and there was deep silence for two miles. Then suddenly he began to sing, very loudly, *H*-A-double-R-*I*-G-A-N *spells Harrr*-i-gan–" She gritted her teeth. She hated that worse than any of his songs except "Barney Google." He would go on to "Barney Google" pretty soon, she knew. Suddenly she leaned slightly forward. The straight line of her lips began to curve up ever so slightly. She heard the safety pins in the tumbler again. Only now they were louder, more insistent, ominous. He was singing too loud to hear them. "Is a *name* that *shame* has never been con-*nec*-ted with–*Harrr*-i-gan, that's *me*!" She relaxed against the back of the seat content to wait.

Arrangement in Black and White

Dorothy Parker

The woman with the pink velvet poppies turned round the assisted gold of her hair traversed the crowded room at an interesting gait combining a skip with a sidle, and clutched the lean arm of her host.

"Now I got you!" she said. "Now you can't get away!"

"Why, hello," said her host. "Well. How are you?"

"Oh, I'm finely," she said. "Just simply finely. Listen. I want you to do me the most terrible favor. Will you? Will you please? Pretty please?"

"What is it?" said her host.

"Listen," she said. "I want to meet Walter Williams. Honestly, I'm just crazy about that man. Oh, when he sings! When he sings those spirituals! Well, I said to Burton, 'It's a good thing for you Walter Williams is colored,' I said, 'or you'd have lots of reason to be jealous.' I'd really love to meet him. I'd like to tell him I've heard him sing. Will you be an angel and introduce me to him?"

"Why, certainly," said her host. "I thought you'd met him. The party's for him. Where is he, anyway?"

"He's over there by the bookcase," she said. "Let's wait till those people get through talking to him. Well, I think you're simply marvelous, giving this perfectly marvelous party for him, and having him meet all these white people, and all. Isn't he terribly grateful?"

"I hope not," said her host.

"I think it's terribly nice," she said. "I do. I don't see why on earth it isn't perfectly all right to meet colored people. I haven't any feeling at all about it—not one single bit. Burton—oh, he's just the other way. Well, you know, he comes from Virginia, and you know how they are."

"Did he come tonight?" said her host.

"No, he couldn't," she said. "I'm a regular grass widow tonight. I told him when I left, 'There's no telling what I'll do,' I said. He was just so tired out, he couldn't move. Isn't it a shame?"

"Ah," said her host.

"Wait till I tell him I met Walter Williams!" she said. "He'll just about die. Oh, we have more arguments about colored people. I talk to him like I don't know what, I get so excited. 'Oh, don't be so silly,' I say. But I must say for Burton, he's heaps broader-minded than lots of these Southerners. He's really awfully fond of colored people. Well, he says himself, he wouldn't have white servants. And you know, he had this old colored nurse, this regular old nigger mammy, and he just simply loves her. Why, every time he goes home, he goes out in the kitchen to see her. He does, really, to this day. All he says is, he says he hasn't got a word to say against colored people as long as they keep their place. He's always doing things for them—giving them clothes and I don't know what all. The only thing he says, he says he wouldn't sit down at the table with one for a million dollars. 'Oh,' I say to him, 'you make me sick, talking like that.' I'm just terrible to him. Aren't I just terrible?"

"Oh, no, no, no," said her host. "No, no."

"I am," she said. "I know I am. Poor Burton! Now, me, I don't feel that way at all. I haven't the slightest feeling about colored people. Why, I'm just crazy about some of them. They're just like children—just as easy-going, and always singing and laughing and everything. Aren't they the happiest things you ever saw in your life? Honestly, it makes me laugh just to hear them. Oh, I like them. I really do. Well, now, listen, I have this colored laundress, I've had her for years, and I'm devoted to her. She's a real character. And I want to tell you, I think of her as my friend. That's the way I think of her. As I say to Burton, 'Well, for Heaven's sakes, we're all human beings!' Aren't we?"

"Yes," said her host. "Yes, indeed."

"Now this Walter Williams," she said. "I think a man like that's a real artist. I do. I think he deserves an awful lot of credit. Goodness, I'm so crazy about music or anything, I don't care *what* color he is. I honestly think if a person's an artist, nobody ought to have any feeling at all about meeting them. That's absolutely what I say to

Burton. Don't you think I'm right?"

"Yes," said her host. "Oh, yes."

"That's the way I feel," she said. "I just can't understand people being narrow-minded. Why, I absolutely think it's a privilege to meet a man like Walter Williams. Yes, I do. I haven't any feeling at all. Well, my goodness, the good Lord made him, just the same as He did any of us. Didn't He?"

"Surely," said her host. "Yes, indeed."

"That's what I say," she said. "Oh, I get so furious when people are narrow-minded about colored people. It's just all I can do not to say something. Of course, I do admit when you get a bad colored man, they're simply terrible. But as I say to Burton, there are some bad white people, too, in this world. Aren't there?"

"I guess there are," said her host.

"Why, I'd really be glad to have a man like Walter Williams come to my house and sing for us, some time," she said. "Of course, I couldn't ask him on account of Burton, but I wouldn't have any feeling about it at all. Oh, can't he sing! Isn't it marvelous, the way they all have music in them? It just seems to be right *in* them. Come on, let's us go on over and talk to him. Listen, what shall I do when I'm introduced? Ought I to shake hands? Or what?"

"Why, do whatever you want," said her host.

"I guess maybe I'd better," she said. "I wouldn't for the world have him think I had any feeling. I think I'd better shake hands, just the way I would with anybody else. That's just exactly what I'll do."

They reached the tall young Negro, standing by the bookcase. The host performed introductions; the Negro bowed.

"How do you do?" he said.

The woman with the pink velvet poppies extended her hand at the length of her arm and held it so for all the world to see, until the Negro took it, shook it, and gave it back to her.

"Oh, how do you do, Mr. Williams," she said. "Well, how do you do. I've just been saying, I've enjoyed your singing so awfully much. I've been to your concerts, and we have you on the phonograph and everything. Oh, I just enjoy it!"

She spoke with great distinctness, moving her lips meticulously, as if in parlance with the deaf.

"I'm so glad," he said.

"I'm just simply crazy about that 'Water Boy' thing you sing," she said. "Honestly, I can't get it out of my head. I have my husband nearly crazy, the way I go around humming it all the time. Oh, he looks just as black as the ace of–Well. Tell me, where on earth do you ever get all those songs of yours? How do you ever get hold of them?"

"Why," he said, "there are so many different–"

"I should think you'd love singing them," she said. "It must be more fun. All those darling old spirituals–oh, I just love them! Well, what are you doing now? Are you still keeping up your singing? Why don't you have another concert, some time?"

"I'm having one the sixteenth of this month," he said.

"Well, I'll be there," she said. "I'll be there, if I possibly can. You can count on me. Goodness, here comes a whole raft of people to talk to you. You're just a regular guest of honor! Oh, who's that girl in white? I've seen her some place."

"That's Katherine Burke," said her host.

"Good Heavens," she said, "is that Katherine Burke? Why, she looks entirely different off the stage. I thought she was much better-looking. I had no idea she was so terribly dark. Why, she looks almost like–Oh, I think she's a wonderful actress! Don't you think she's a wonderful actress, Mr. Williams? Oh, I think she's marvelous. Don't you?"

"Yes, I do," he said.

"Oh, I do, too," she said. "Just wonderful. Well, goodness, we must give someone else a chance to talk–to the guest of honor. Now, don't forget, Mr. Williams, I'm going to be at that concert if I possibly can. I'll be there applauding like everything. And if I can't come, I'm going to tell everybody I know to go, anyway. Don't you forget!"

"I won't," he said. "Thank you so much."

The host took her arm and piloted her into the next room.

"Oh, my dear," she said. "I nearly died! Honestly, I give you my word, I nearly passed away. Did you hear that terrible break I made? I was just going to say Katherine Burke looked almost like a nigger. I just caught myself in time. Oh, do you think he noticed?"

"I don't believe so," said her host.

"Well, thank goodness," she said, "because I wouldn't have embarrassed him for anything. Why, he's awfully nice. Just as nice as he can be. Nice manners, and everything. You know, so many colored people, you give them an inch, and they walk all over you. But he doesn't try any of that. Well, he's got more sense, I suppose. He's really nice. Don't you think so?"

"Yes," said her host.

"I liked him," she said. "I haven't any feeling at all because he's a colored man. I felt just as natural as I would with anybody. Talked to him just as naturally, and everything. But honestly, I could hardly keep a straight face. I kept thinking of Burton. Oh, wait till I tell Burton I called him 'Mister'!"

Coffee Break

Langston Hughes

"My boss is white," said Simple.

"Most bosses are," I said.

"And being white and curious, my boss keeps asking me just what does *the* Negro want. Yesterday he tackled me during the coffee break, talking about *the* Negro. He always says '*the* Negro,' as if there was not 50-11 different kinds of Negroes in the U.S.A.," complained Simple. "My boss says, 'Now that you-all have got the Civil Rights Bill and the Supreme Court, Adam Powell in Congress, Ralph Bunche in the United Nations, and Leontyne Price singing in the Metropolitan Opera, plus Dr. Martin Luther King getting the Nobel Prize, what more do you want? I am asking you, just what does *the* Negro want?'

" 'I am not *the* Negro,' I says. 'I am *me*.'

" 'Well,' says my boss, 'you represent *the* Negro.'

" 'I do not,' I says. 'I represent my own self.'

" 'Ralph Bunche represents you, then,' says my boss, 'and Thurgood Marshall and Martin Luther King. Do they not?'

" 'I am proud to be represented by such men, if you say they represent me,' I said. 'But all them men you name are *way* up there, and they do not drink beer in my bar. I have never seen a single one of them mens on Lenox Avenue in my natural life. So far as I know, they do not even live in Harlem. I cannot find them in the telephone book. They all got private numbers. But since you say they represent *the* Negro, why do you not ask them what *the* Negro wants?'

" 'I cannot get to them,' says my boss.

" 'Neither can I,' I says, 'so we both is in the same boat.'

" 'Well then, to come nearer home,' says my boss, 'Roy Wilkins fights your battles, also James Farmer.'

" 'They do not drink in my bar, neither,' I said.

" 'Don't Wilkins and Farmer live in Harlem?' he asked.

" 'Not to my knowledge,' I said. 'And I bet they have not been to the Apollo since Jackie Mabley cracked the first joke.'

" 'I do not know him,' said my boss, 'but I see Nipsey Russell and Bill Cosby on TV.'

" 'Jackie Mabley is no *him*,' I said. 'She is a *she*—better known as Moms.'

" 'Oh,' said my boss.

" 'And Moms Mabley has a story on one of her records about Little Cindy Ella and the magic slippers going to the Junior Prom at Ole Miss which tells all about what the Negro wants.'

" 'What's its conclusion?' asked my boss.

" 'When the clock strikes midnight, Little Cindy Ella is dancing with the President of the Ku Klux Klan, says Moms, but at the stroke of twelve, Cindy Ella turns back to her natural self, black, and her blonde wig turns to a stocking cap—and her trial comes up next week.'

" 'A symbolic tale,' says my boss, 'meaning, I take it, that *the* Negro is in jail. But you are not in jail.'

" 'That's what you think,' I said.

" 'Anyhow, you claim you are not *the* Negro,' said my boss.

" 'I am not,' I said, 'I am *this* Negro.'

" 'Then what do *you* want?' asked my boss.

" 'To get out of jail,' I said.

" 'What jail?'

" 'The jail you got me in.'

" 'Me?' yells my boss. 'I have not got you in jail. Why, boy, I like you. I am a liberal. I voted for Kennedy. And this time for Johnson. I believe in integration. Now that you got it, though, what more do you want?'

" 'Reintegration,' I said.

" 'Meaning by that, what?'

" 'That you be integrated with *me*, not me with you.'

" 'Do you mean that I come and live in Harlem?' asked my boss. 'Never!'

" 'I live in Harlem,' I said.

" 'You are adjusted to it,' said my boss. 'But there is so much crime in Harlem.'

" 'There are no two-hundred-thousand-dollar bank robberies, though,' I said, 'of which there was three lately *elsewhere*—all done by white folks, and nary one in Harlem. The biggest and best crime is outside of Harlem. We never has no half-million-dollar jewelry robberies, no missing star sapphires. You better come uptown with me and reintegrate.'

" 'Negroes are the ones who want to be integrated,' said my boss.

" 'And white folks are the ones who do *not* want to be,' I said.

" 'Up to a point, we do,' said my boss.

" 'That is what *the* Negro wants,' I said, 'to remove that *point*.'

" 'The coffee break is over,' said my boss."

The Bride Comes to Yellow Sky

Stephen Crane

I

The great Pullman was whirling onward with such dignity of motion that a glance from the window seemed simply to prove that the plains of Texas were pouring eastward. Vast flats of green grass, dull-hued spaces of mesquit and cactus, little groups of frame houses, woods of light and tender trees, all were sweeping into the east, sweeping over the horizon, a precipice.

A newly married pair had boarded this coach at San Antonio. The man's face was reddened from many days in the wind and sun, and a direct result of his new black clothes was that his brick-coloured hands were constantly performing in a most conscious fashion. From time to time he looked down respectfully at his attire. He sat with a hand on each knee, like a man waiting in a barber's shop. The glances he devoted to other passengers were furtive and shy.

The bride was not pretty, nor was she very young. She wore a dress of blue cashmere, with small reservations of velvet here and there, and with steel buttons abounding. She continually twisted her head to regard her puff sleeves, very stiff, straight, and high. They embarrassed her. It was quite apparent that she had cooked, and that she expected to cook, dutifully. The blushes caused by the careless scrutiny of some passengers as she had entered the car were strange to see upon this plain, under-class countenance, which was drawn in placid, almost emotionless lines.

They were evidently very happy. "Ever been in a parlour-car

before?" he asked, smiling with delight.

"No," she answered; "I never was. It's fine, ain't it?"

"Great! And then after a while we'll go forward to the diner, and get a big lay-out. Finest meal in the world. Charge a dollar."

"Oh, do they?" cried the bride. "Charge a dollar? Why, that's too much—for us—ain't it, Jack?"

"Not this trip, anyhow," he answered bravely. "We're going to go the whole thing."

Later he explained to her about the trains. "You see, it's a thousand miles from one end of Texas to the other; and this train runs right across it, and never stops but four times." He had the pride of an owner. He pointed out to her the dazzling fittings of the coach; and in truth her eyes opened wider as she contemplated the sea-green figured velvet, the shining brass, silver, and glass, the wood that gleamed as darkly brilliant as the surface of a pool of oil. At one end a bronze figure sturdily held a support for a separated chamber, and at convenient places on the ceiling were frescos in olive and silver.

To the minds of the pair, their surroundings reflected the glory of their marriage that morning in San Antonio; this was the environment of their new estate; and the man's face in particular beamed with an elation that made him appear ridiculous to the negro porter. This individual at times surveyed them from afar with an amused and superior grin. On other occasions he bullied them with skill in ways that did not make it exactly plain to them that they were being bullied. He subtly used all the manners of the most unconquerable kind of snobbery. He oppressed them; but of this oppression they had small knowledge, and they speedily forgot that infrequently a number of travellers covered them with stares of derisive enjoyment. Historically there was supposed to be something infinitely humorous in their situation.

"We are due in Yellow Sky at 3:42," he said, looking tenderly into her eyes.

"Oh, are we?" she said, as if she had not been aware of it. To evince surprise at her husband's statement was part of her wifely amiability. She took from a pocket a little silver watch; and as she held it before her, and stared at it with a frown of attention, the new husband's face shone.

"I bought it in San Anton' from a friend of mine," he told her gleefully.

"It's seventeen minutes past twelve," she said, looking up at him with a kind of shy and clumsy coquetry. A passenger, noting this play, grew excessively sardonic, and winked at himself in one of the numerous mirrors.

At last they went to the dining-car. Two rows of negro waiters, in glowing white suits, surveyed their entrance with the interest, and also the equanimity, of men who had been forewarned. The pair fell to the lot of a waiter who happened to feel pleasure in steering them through their meal. He viewed them with the manner of a fatherly pilot, his countenance radiant with benevolence. The patronage, entwined with the ordinary deference, was not plain to them. And yet, as they returned to their coach, they showed in their faces a sense of escape.

To the left, miles down a long purple slope, was a little ribbon of mist where moved the keening Rio Grande. The train was approaching it at an angle, and the apex was Yellow Sky. Presently it was apparent that, as the distance from Yellow Sky grew shorter, the husband became commensurately restless. His brick-red hands were more insistent in their prominence. Occasionally he was even rather absent-minded and far-away when the bride leaned forward and addressed him.

As a matter of truth, Jack Potter was beginning to find the shadow of a deed weigh upon him like a leaden slab. He, the town marshal of Yellow Sky, a man known, liked, and feared in his corner, a prominent person, had gone to San Antonio to meet a girl he believed he loved, and there, after the usual prayers, had actually induced her to marry him, without consulting Yellow Sky for any part of the transaction. He was now bringing his bride before an innocent and unsuspecting community.

Of course people in Yellow Sky married as it pleased them, in accordance with a general custom; but such was Potter's thought of his duty to his friends, or of their idea of his duty, or of an unspoken form which does not control men in these matters, that he felt he was heinous. He had committed an extraordinary crime. Face to face with this girl in San Antonio, and spurred by his sharp impulse, he had gone headlong over all the social hedges. At San Antonio he was like a man hidden in the dark. A knife to sever any friendly duty, any form, was easy to his hand in that remote city. But the hour of Yellow Sky—the hour of daylight—was approaching.

He knew full well that his marriage was an important thing to his town. It could only be exceeded by the burning of the new hotel. His friends could not forgive him. Frequently he had reflected on the advisability of telling them by telegraph, but a new cowardice had been upon him. He feared to do it. And now the train was hurrying him toward a scene of amazement, glee, and reproach. He glanced out of the window at the line of haze swinging slowly in toward the train.

Yellow Sky had a kind of brass band, which played painfully, to the delight of the populace. He laughed without heart as he thought of it. If the citizens could dream of his prospective arrival with his bride, they would parade the band at the station and escort them, amid cheers and laughing congratulations, to his adobe home.

He resolved that he would use all the devices of speed and plainscraft in making the journey from the station to his house. Once within that safe citadel, he could issue some sort of vocal bulletin, and then not go among the citizens until they had time to wear off a little of their enthusiasm.

The bride looked anxiously at him. "What's worrying you, Jack?"

He laughed again. "I'm not worrying, girl; I'm only thinking of Yellow Sky."

She flushed in comprehension.

A sense of mutual guilt invaded their minds and developed a finer tenderness. They looked at each other with eyes softly aglow. But Potter often laughed the same nervous laugh; the flush upon the bride's face seemed quite permanent.

The traitor to the feelings of Yellow Sky narrowly watched the speeding landscape. "We're nearly there," he said.

Presently the porter came and announced the proximity of Potter's home. He held a brush in his hand, and, with all his airy superiority gone, he brushed Potter's new clothes as the latter slowly turned this way and that way. Potter fumbled out a coin and gave it to the porter, as he had seen others do. It was a heavy and muscle-bound business, as that of a man shoeing his first horse.

The porter took their bag, and as the train began to slow they moved forward to the hooded platform of the car. Presently the two engines and their long string of coaches rushed into the station of Yellow Sky.

"They have to take water here," said Potter, from a constricted throat and in mournful cadence, as one announcing death. Before the train stopped his eye had swept the length of the platform, and he was glad and astonished to see there was none upon it but the station-agent, who, with a slightly hurried and anxious air, was walking toward the water-tanks. When the train had halted, the porter alighted first, and placed in position a little temporary step.

"Come on, girl," said Potter, hoarsely. As he helped her down they each laughed on a false note. He took the bag from the negro, and bade his wife cling to his arm. As they slunk rapidly away, his hang-dog glance perceived that they were unloading the two trunks, and also that the station-agent, far ahead near the baggage-car, had turned and was running toward him, making gestures. He laughed, and groaned as he laughed, when he noted the first effect of his marital bliss upon Yellow Sky. He gripped his wife's arm firmly to his side, and they fled. Behind them the porter stood, chuckling fatuously.

II

The California express on the Southern Railway was due at Yellow Sky in twenty-one minutes. There were six men at the bar of the Weary Gentleman saloon. One was a drummer who talked a great deal and rapidly; three were Texans who did not care to talk at that time; and two were Mexican sheepherders, who did not talk as a general practice in the Weary Gentleman saloon. The barkeeper's dog lay on the board walk that crossed in front of the door. His head was on his paws, and he glanced drowsily here and there with the constant vigilance of a dog that is kicked on occasion. Across the sandy street were some vivid green grass-plots, so wonderful in appearance, amid the sands that burned near them in a blazing sun, that they caused a doubt in the mind. They exactly resembled the grass mats used to represent lawns on the stage. At the cooler end of the railway station, a man without a coat sat in a tilted chair and smoked his pipe. The fresh-cut bank of the Rio Grande circled near the town, and there could be seen beyond it a great plum-coloured plain of mesquit.

Save for the busy drummer and his companions in the saloon, Yellow Sky was dozing. The new-comer leaned gracefully upon the bar, and recited many tales with the confidence of a bard who has come upon a new field.

"—and at the moment that the old man fell downstairs with the bureau in his arms, the old woman was coming up with two scuttles of coal, and of course—"

The drummer's tale was interrupted by a young man who suddenly appeared in the open door. He cried: "Scratchy Wilson's drunk, and has turned loose with both hands." The two Mexicans at once set down their glasses and faded out of the rear entrance of the saloon.

The drummer, innocent and jocular, answered: "All right, old man. S'pose he has? Come in and have a drink, anyhow."

But the information had made such an obvious cleft in every skull in the room that the drummer was obliged to see its importance. All had become instantly solemn. "Say," said he, mystified, "what is this?" His three companions made the introductory gesture of eloquent speech; but the young man at the door forestalled them.

"It means, my friend," he answered, as he came into the saloon, "that for the next two hours this town won't be a health resort."

The barkeeper went to the door, and locked and barred it; reaching out of the window, he pulled in heavy wooden shutters, and barred them. Immediately a solemn, chapel-like gloom was upon the place. The drummer was looking from one to another.

"But say," he cried, "what is this, anyhow? You don't mean there is going to be a gun-fight?"

"Don't know whether there'll be a fight or not," answered one man, grimly; "but there'll be some shootin'—some good shootin'."

The young man who had warned them waved his hand. "Oh, there'll be a fight fast enough, if any one wants it. Anybody can get a fight out there in the street. There's a fight just waiting."

The drummer seemed to be swayed between the interest of a foreigner and a perception of personal danger.

"What did you say his name was?" he asked.

"Scratchy Wilson," they answered in chorus.

"And will he kill anybody? What are you going to do? Does this happen often? Does he rampage around like this once a week or so? Can he break in that door?"

"No; he can't break down that door," replied the barkeeper. "He's tried it three times. But when he comes you'd better lay down on the floor, stranger. He's dead sure to shoot at it, and a bullet may come through."

Thereafter the drummer kept a strict eye upon the door. The time had not yet been called for him to hug the floor, but, as a minor precaution, he sidled near to the wall. "Will he kill anybody?" he said again.

The men laughed low and scornfully at the question.

"He's out to shoot, and he's out for trouble. Don't see any good in experimentin' with him."

"But what do you do in a case like this? What do you do?"

A man responded: "Why, he and Jack Potter–"

"But," in chorus the other men interrupted, "Jack Potter's in San Anton'."

"Well, who is he? What's he got to do with it?"

"Oh, he's the town marshal. He goes out and fights Scratchy when he gets on one of these tears."

"Wow!" said the drummer, mopping his brow. "Nice job he's got."

The voices had toned away to mere whisperings. The drummer wished to ask further questions, which were born of an increasing anxiety and bewilderment; but when he attempted them, the men merely looked at him in irritation and motioned him to remain silent. A tense waiting hush was upon them. In the deep shadows of the room their eyes shone as they listened for sounds from the street. One man made three gestures at the barkeeper; and the latter, moving like a ghost, handed him a glass and a bottle. The man poured a full glass of whisky, and set down the bottle noiselessly. He gulped the whisky in a swallow, and turned again toward the door in immovable silence. The drummer saw that the barkeeper, without a sound, had taken a Winchester from beneath the bar. Later he saw this individual beckoning to him, so he tiptoed across the room.

"You better come with me back of the bar."

"No, thanks," said the drummer, perspiring; "I'd rather be where I can make a break for the back door."

Whereupon the man of bottles made a kindly but peremptory gesture. The drummer obeyed it, and, finding himself seated on a box with his head below the level of the bar, balm was laid upon his soul at sight of various zinc and copper fittings that bore a resemblance to armour-plate. The barkeeper took a seat comfortably upon an adjacent box.

"You see," he whispered, "this here Scratchy Wilson is a wonder with a gun–a perfect wonder; and when he goes on the war-trail, we hunt our holes–naturally. He's about the last one of the old gang that used to hang out along the river here. He's a terror when he's drunk. When he's sober he's all right–kind of simple–wouldn't hurt a fly–nicest fellow in town. But when he's drunk–whoo!"

There were periods of stillness. "I wish Jack Potter was back from San Anton'," said the barkeeper. "He shot Wilson up once–in the leg–and he would sail in and pull out the kinks in this thing."

Presently they heard from a distance the sound of a shot, followed by three wild yowls. It instantly removed a bond from the men in the darkened saloon. There was a shuffling of feet. They looked at each other. "Here he comes," they said.

III

A man in a maroon-coloured flannel shirt, which had been purchased for purposes of decoration, and made principally by some Jewish women on the East Side of New York, rounded a corner and walked into the middle of the main street of Yellow Sky. In either hand the man held a long, heavy, blue-black revolver. Often he yelled, and these cries rang through a semblance of a deserted village, shrilly flying over the roofs in a volume that seemed to have no relation to the ordinary vocal strength of a man. It was as if the surrounding stillness formed the arch of a tomb over him. These cries of ferocious challenge rang against walls of silence. And his boots had red tops with gilded imprints, of the kind beloved in winter by little sledding boys on the hillsides of New England.

The man's face flamed in a rage begot of whisky. His eyes, rolling, and yet keen for ambush, hunted the still doorways and windows. He walked with the creeping movement of the midnight cat. As it occurred to him, he roared menacing information. The long revolvers in his hands were as easy as straws; they were moved with an electric swiftness. The little fingers of each hand played sometimes in a musician's way. Plain from the low collar of the shirt, the cords of his neck straightened and sank, straightened and sank, as passion moved him. The only sounds were his terrible invitations. The calm adobes preserved their demeanour at the passing of this small thing in the middle of the street.

There was no offer of fight–no offer of fight. The man called to the sky. There were no attractions. He bellowed and fumed and swayed his revolvers here and everywhere.

The dog of the barkeeper of the Weary Gentleman saloon had not appreciated the advance of events. He yet lay dozing in front of his master's door. At sight of the dog, the man paused and raised his revolver humorously. At sight of the man, the dog sprang up and walked diagonally away, with a sullen head, and growling. The man yelled, and the dog broke into a gallop. As it was about to enter an alley, there was a loud noise, a whistling, and something spat the ground directly before it. The dog screamed, and, wheeling in terror, galloped headlong in a new direction. Again there was a noise, a whistling, and sand was kicked viciously before it. Fear-stricken, the dog turned and flurried like an animal in a pen. The man stood laughing, his weapons at his hips.

Ultimately the man was attracted by the closed door of the Weary Gentleman saloon. He went to it and, hammering with a revolver, demanded drink.

The door remaining imperturbable, he picked a bit of paper from the walk, and nailed it to the framework with a knife. He then turned his back contemptuously upon this popular resort and, walking to the opposite side of the street and spinning there on his heel quickly and lithely, fired at the bit of paper. He missed it by a half-inch. He swore at himself, and went away. Later he comfortably fusilladed the windows of his most intimate friend. The man was playing with this town; it was a toy for him.

But still there was no offer of fight. The name of Jack Potter, his ancient antagonist, entered his mind, and he concluded that it would be a glad thing if he should go to Potter's house, and by bombardment induce him to come out and fight. He moved in the direction of his desire, chanting Apache scalp-music.

When he arrived at it, Potter's house presented the same still front as had the other adobes. Taking up a strategic position, the man howled a challenge. But this house regarded him as might a great stone god. It gave no sign. After a decent wait, the man howled further challenges, mingling with them wonderful epithets.

Presently there came the spectacle of a man churning himself into deepest rage over the immobility of a house. He fumed at it as the winter wind attacks a prairie cabin in the North. To the distance there should have gone the sound of a tumult like the fighting of two hundred Mexicans. As necessity bade him, he paused for breath or to reload his revolvers.

IV

Potter and his bride walked sheepishly and with speed. Sometimes they laughed together shamefacedly and low.

"Next corner, dear," he said finally.

They put forth the efforts of a pair walking bowed against a strong wind. Potter was about to raise a finger to point the first appearance of the new home when, as they circled the corner, they came face to face with a man in a maroon-coloured shirt, who was feverishly pushing cartridges into a large revolver. Upon the instant the man dropped his revolver to the ground and, like lightning, whipped another from its holster. The second weapon was aimed at the bridegroom's chest.

There was a silence. Potter's mouth seemed to be merely a grave for his tongue. He exhibited an instinct to at once loosen his arm from the woman's grip, and he dropped the bag to the sand. As for the bride, her face had gone as yellow as old cloth. She was a slave to hideous rites, gazing at the apparitional snake.

The two men faced each other at a distance of three paces. He of the revolver smiled with a new and quiet ferocity.

"Tried to sneak up on me," he said. "Tried to sneak up on me!" His eyes grew more baleful. As Potter made a slight movement, the man thrust his revolver venomously forward. "No; don't you do it, Jack Potter. Don't you move a finger toward a gun just yet. Don't you move an eyelash. The time has come for me to settle with you, and I'm goin' to do it my own way, and loaf along with no interferin'. So if you don't want a gun bent on you, just mind what I tell you."

Potter looked at his enemy. "I ain't got a gun on me Scratchy," he said. "Honest, I ain't." He was stiffening and steadying, but yet somewhere at the back of his mind a vision of the Pullman floated: the sea-green figured velvet, the shining brass, silver, and glass, the wood that gleamed as darkly brilliant as the surface of a pool of oil—all the glory of the marriage, the environment of the new estate. "You know I fight when it comes to fighting, Scratchy Wilson; but I ain't got a gun on me. You'll have to do all the shootin' yourself."

His enemy's face went livid. He stepped forward, and lashed his weapon to and fro before Potter's chest. "Don't you tell me you ain't got no gun on you, you whelp. Don't tell me no lie like that. There ain't a man in Texas ever seen you without no gun. Don't take me for no kid." His eyes blazed with light, and his throat worked like a pump.

"I ain't takin' you for no kid," answered Potter. His heels had not moved an inch backward. "I'm takin' you for a damn fool. I tell you

I ain't got a gun, and I ain't. If you're goin' to shoot me up, you better begin now; you'll never get a chance like this again."

So much enforced reasoning had told on Wilson's rage; he was calmer. "If you ain't got a gun, why ain't you got a gun?" he sneered. "Been to Sunday-school?"

"I ain't got a gun because I've just come from San Anton' with my wife. I'm married," said Potter. "And if I'd thought there was going to be any galoots like you prowling around when I brought my wife home, I'd had a gun, and don't you forget it."

"Married!" said Scratchy, not at all comprehending.

"Yes, married. I'm married," said Potter, distinctly.

"Married?" said Scratchy. Seemingly for the first time, he saw the drooping, drowning woman at the other man's side. "No!" he said. He was like a creature allowed a glimpse of another world. He moved a pace backward, and his arm, with the revolver, dropped to his side. "Is this the lady?" he asked.

"Yes; this is the lady," answered Potter.

There was another period of silence.

"Well," said Wilson at last, slowly, "I s'pose it's all off now."

"It's all off if you say so, Scratchy. You know I didn't make the trouble." Potter lifted his valise.

"Well, I 'low it's off, Jack," said Wilson. He was looking at the ground. "Married!" He was not a student of chivalry; it was merely that in the presence of this foreign condition he was a simple child of the earlier plains. He picked up his starboard revolver, and, placing both weapons in their holsters, he went away. His feet made funnel-shaped tracks in the heavy sand.

Harrison Bergeron

Kurt Vonnegut, Jr.

The year was 2081, and everybody was finally equal. They weren't only equal before God and the law. They were equal every which way. Nobody was smarter than anybody else. Nobody was better looking than anybody else. Nobody was stronger or quicker than anybody else. All this equality was due to the 211th, 212th, and 213th Amendments to the Constitution, and to the unceasing vigilance of agents of the United States Handicapper General.

Some things about living still weren't quite right, though. April, for instance, still drove people crazy by not being springtime. And it was in that clammy month that the H-G men took George and Hazel Bergeron's fourteen-year-old son, Harrison, away.

It was tragic, all right, but George and Hazel couldn't think about it very hard. Hazel had a perfectly average intelligence, which meant she couldn't think about anything except in short bursts. And George, while his intelligence was way above normal, had a little mental handicap radio in his ear. He was required by law to wear it at all times. It was tuned to a government transmitter. Every twenty seconds or so, the transmitter would send out some sharp noise to keep people like George from taking unfair advantage of their brains.

George and Hazel were watching television. There were tears on Hazel's cheeks, but she'd forgotten for the moment what they were about.

On the television screen were ballerinas.

A buzzer sounded in George's head. His thoughts fled in panic, like bandits from a burglar alarm.

"That was a real pretty dance, that dance they just did," said Hazel.

"Huh?" said George.

"That dance—it was nice," said Hazel.

"Yup," said George. He tried to think a little about the ballerinas. They weren't really very good—no better than anybody else would have been, anyway. They were burdened with sashweights and bags of birdshot, and their faces were masked, so that no one, seeing a free and graceful gesture or a pretty face, would feel like something the cat drug in. George was toying with the vague notion that maybe dancers shouldn't be handicapped. But he didn't get very far with it before another noise in his ear radio scattered his thoughts.

George winced. So did two out of the eight ballerinas.

Hazel saw him wince. Having no mental handicap herself, she had to ask George what the latest sound had been.

"Sounded like somebody hitting a milk bottle with a ball peen hammer," said George.

"I'd think it would be real interesting, hearing all the different sounds," said Hazel, a little envious. "All the things they think up."

"Um," said George.

"Only, if I was Handicapper General, you know what I would do?" said Hazel. Hazel, as a matter of fact, bore a strong resemblance to the Handicapper General, a woman named Diana Moon Glampers. "If I was Diana Moon Glampers," said Hazel, "I'd have chimes on Sunday—just chimes. Kind of in honor of religion."

"I could think, if it was just chimes," said George.

"Well—maybe make 'em real loud," said Hazel. "I think I'd make a good Handicapper General."

"Good as anybody else," said George.

"Who knows better'n I do what normal is?" said Hazel.

"Right," said George. He began to think glimmeringly about his abnormal son who was now in jail, about Harrison, but a twenty-one-gun salute in his head stopped that.

"Boy!" said Hazel, "that was a doozy, wasn't it?"

It was such a doozy that George was white and trembling, and tears stood on the rims of his red eyes. Two of the eight ballerinas had collapsed to the studio floor, were holding their temples.

"All of a sudden you look so tired," said Hazel. "Why don't you stretch out on the sofa, so's you can rest your handicap bag on the pillows, honeybunch." She was referring to the forty-seven pounds of birdshot in a canvas bag, which was padlocked around George's neck. "Go on and rest the bag for a little while," she said. "I don't care if you're not equal to me for a while."

George weighed the bag with his hands. "I don't mind it," he said. "I don't notice it any more. It's just a part of me."

"You been so tired lately–kind of wore out," said Hazel. "If there was just some way we could make a little hole in the bottom of the bag, and just take out a few of them lead balls. Just a few."

"Two years in prison and two thousand dollars fine for every ball I took out," said George. "I don't call that a bargain."

"If you could just take a few out when you came home from work," said Hazel. "I mean–you don't compete with anybody around here. You just set around."

"If I tried to get away with it," said George, "then other people'd get away with it–and pretty soon we'd be right back to the dark ages again, with everybody competing against everybody else. You wouldn't like that, would you?"

"I'd hate it," said Hazel.

"There you are," said George. "The minute people start cheating on laws, what do you think happens to society?"

If Hazel hadn't been able to come up with an answer to this question, George couldn't have supplied one. A siren was going off in his head.

"Reckon it'd fall all apart," said Hazel.

"What would?" said George blankly.

"Society," said Hazel uncertainly. "Wasn't that what you just said?"

"Who knows?" said George.

The television program was suddenly interrupted for a news bulletin. It wasn't clear at first as to what the bulletin was about, since the announcer, like all announcers, had a serious speech impediment. For about half a minute, and in a state of high excitement, the announcer tried to say, "Ladies and gentlemen–"

He finally gave up, handed the bulletin to a ballerina to read.

"That's all right–" Hazel said of the announcer, "he tried. That's the big thing. He tried to do the best he could with what God gave him. He should get a nice raise for trying so hard."

"Ladies and gentlemen–" said the ballerina, reading the bulletin. She must have been extraordinarily beautiful, because the mask she wore was hideous. And it was easy to see that she was the strongest and most graceful of all the dancers, for her handicap bags were as big as those worn by two-hundred-pound men.

And she had to apologize at once for her voice, which was a very unfair voice for a woman to use. Her voice was a warm, luminous, timeless melody. "Excuse me–" she said, and she began again, making her voice absolutely uncompetitive.

"Harrison Bergeron, age fourteen," she said in a grackle squawk, "has just escaped from jail, where he was held on suspicion of plotting to overthrow the government. He is a genius and an athlete, is under-handicapped, and should be regarded as extremely dangerous."

A police photograph of Harrison Bergeron was flashed on the screen–upside down, then sideways, upside down again, then right side up. The picture showed the full length of Harrison against a background calibrated in feet and inches. He was exactly seven feet tall.

The rest of Harrison's appearance was Halloween and hardware. Nobody had ever borne heavier handicaps. He had outgrown hindrances faster than the H-G men could think them up. Instead of a little ear radio for a mental handicap, he wore a tremendous pair of earphones, and spectacles with thick wavy lenses. The spectacles were intended to make him not only half blind, but to give him whanging headaches besides.

Scrap metal was hung all over him. Ordinarily, there was a certain symmetry, a military neatness to the handicaps issued to strong people, but Harrison looked like a walking junkyard. In the race of life, Harrison carried three hundred pounds.

And to offset his good looks, the H-G men required that he wear at all times a red rubber ball for a nose, keep his eyebrows shaved off, and cover his even white teeth with black caps at snaggle-tooth random.

"If you see this boy," said the ballerina, "do not–I repeat, do not–try to reason with him."

There was the shriek of a door being torn from its hinges.

Screams and barking cries of consternation came from the television set. The photograph of Harrison Bergeron on the screen jumped again and again, as though dancing to the tune of an earthquake.

George Bergeron correctly identified the earthquake, and well he might have–for many was the time his own home had danced to the same crashing tune. "My God–" said George, "that must be Harrison!"

The realization was blasted from his mind instantly by the sound of an automobile collision in his head.

When George could open his eyes again, the photograph of Harrison was gone. A living, breathing Harrison filled the screen.

Clanking, clownish, and huge, Harrison stood in the center of the studio. The knob of the uprooted studio door was still in his hand. Ballerinas, technicians, musicians, and announcers cowered on their knees before him, expecting to die.

"I am the Emperor!" cried Harrison. "Do you hear? I am the Emperor! Everybody must do what I say at once!" He stamped his foot and the studio shook.

"Even as I stand here—" he bellowed, "crippled, hobbled, sickened—I am a greater ruler than any man who ever lived! Now watch me become what I *can* become!"

Harrison tore the straps of his handicap harness like wet tissue paper, tore straps guaranteed to support five thousand pounds.

Harrison's scrap-iron handicaps crashed to the floor.

Harrison thrust his thumbs under the bar of the padlock that secured his head harness. The bar snapped like celery. Harrison smashed his headphones and spectacles against the wall.

He flung away his rubber-ball nose, revealed a man that would have awed Thor, the god of thunder.

"I shall now select my Empress!" he said, looking down on the cowering people. "Let the first woman who dares rise to her feet claim her mate and her throne!"

A moment passed, and then a ballerina arose, swaying like a willow.

Harrison plucked the mental handicap from her ear, snapped off her physical handicaps with marvelous delicacy. Last of all, he removed her mask.

She was blindingly beautiful.

"Now—" said Harrison, taking her hand, "shall we show the people the meaning of the word dance? Music!" he commanded.

The musicians scrambled back into their chairs, and Harrison stripped them of their handicaps, too. "Play your best," he told them, "and I'll make you barons and dukes and earls."

The music began. It was normal at first—cheap, silly, false. But Harrison snatched two musicians from their chairs, waved them like batons as he sang the music as he wanted it played. He slammed them back into their chairs.

The music began again and was much improved.

Harrison and his Empress merely listened to the music for a while—listened gravely, as though synchronizing their heartbeats with it.

They shifted their weights to their toes.

Harrison placed his big hands on the girl's tiny waist, letting her sense the weightlessness that would soon be hers.

And then, in an explosion of joy and grace, into the air they sprang!

Not only were the laws of the land abandoned, but the law of gravity and the laws of motion as well.

They reeled, whirled, swiveled, flounced, capered, gamboled, and spun.

They leaped like deer on the moon.

The studio ceiling was thirty feet high, but each leap brought the dancers nearer to it.

It became their obvious intention to kiss the ceiling.

They kissed it.

And then, neutralizing gravity with love and pure will, they remained suspended in air inches below the ceiling, and they kissed each other for a long, long time.

It was then that Diana Moon Glampers, the Handicapper General, came into the studio with a double-barreled ten-gauge shotgun. She fired twice, and the Emperor and the Empress were dead before they hit the floor.

Diana Moon Glampers loaded the gun again. She aimed it at the musicians and told them they had ten seconds to get their handicaps back on.

It was then that the Bergerons' television tube burned out.

Hazel turned to comment about the blackout to George. But George had gone out into the kitchen for a can of beer.

George came back in with the beer, paused while a handicap signal shook him up. And then he sat down again. "You been crying?" he said to Hazel.

"Yup," she said.

"What about?" he said.

"I forget," she said. "Something real sad on television."

"What was it?" he said.

"It's all kind of mixed up in my mind," said Hazel.

"Forget sad things," said George.

"I always do," said Hazel.

"That's my girl," said George. He winced. There was the sound of a rivetting gun in his head.

"Gee—I could tell that one was a doozy," said Hazel.

"You can say that again," said George.

"Gee—" said Hazel, "I could tell that one was a doozy."

The Use of Force

William Carlos Williams

They were new patients to me, all I had was the name, Olson. Please come down as soon as you can, my daughter is very sick.

When I arrived I was met by the mother, a big startled looking woman, very clean and apologetic who merely said, Is this the doctor? and let me in. In the back, she added. You must excuse us, doctor, we have her in the kitchen where it is warm. It is very damp here sometimes.

The child was fully dressed and sitting on her father's lap near the kitchen table. He tried to get up, but I motioned for him not to bother, took off my overcoat and started to look things over. I could see that they were all very nervous, eyeing me up and down distrustfully. As often, in such cases, they weren't telling me more than they had to, it was up to me to tell them; that's why they were spending three dollars on me.

The child was fairly eating me up with her cold, steady eyes, and no expression to her face whatever. She did not move and seemed, inwardly, quiet; an unusually attractive little thing, and as strong as a heifer in appearance. But her face was flushed, she was breathing rapidly, and I realized that she had a high fever. She had magnificent blonde hair, in profusion. One of those picture children often reproduced in advertising leaflets and the photogravure sections of the Sunday papers.

She's had a fever for three days, began the father and we don't know what it comes from. My wife has given her things, you know, like people do, but it don't do no good. And there's been a lot of sickness around. So we tho't you'd better look her over and tell us what is the matter.

As doctors often do I took a trial shot at it as a point of departure. Has she had a sore throat?

Both parents answered me together, No . . . No, she says her throat don't hurt her.

Does your throat hurt you? added the mother to the child. But the little girl's expression didn't change nor did she move her eyes from my face.

Have you looked?

I tried to, said the mother, but I couldn't see.

As it happens we had been having a number of cases of diphtheria in the school to which this child went during that month and we were all, quite apparently, thinking of that, though no one had as yet spoken of the thing.

Well, I said, suppose we take a look at the throat first. I smiled in my best professional manner and asking for the child's first name I said, come on, Mathilda, open your mouth and let's take a look at your throat.

Nothing doing.

Aw, come on, I coaxed, just open your mouth wide and let me take a look. Look, I said opening both hands wide, I haven't anything in my hands. Just open up and let me see.

Such a nice man, put in the mother. Look how kind he is to you. Come on, do what he tells you to. He won't hurt you.

At that I ground my teeth in disgust. If only they wouldn't use the word "hurt" I might be able to get somewhere. But I did not allow myself to be hurried or disturbed but speaking quietly and slowly I approached the child again.

As I moved my chair a little nearer suddenly with one catlike movement both her hands clawed instinctively for my eyes and she almost reached them too. In fact she knocked my glasses flying and they fell, though unbroken, several feet away from me on the kitchen floor.

Both the mother and father almost turned themselves inside out in embarrassment and apology. You bad girl, said the mother, taking her and shaking her by one arm. Look what you've done. The nice man . . .

For heaven's sake, I broke in. Don't call me a nice man to her. I'm here to look at her throat on the chance that she might have diphtheria and possibly die of it. But that's nothing to her. Look here, I said to the child, we're going to look at your throat. You're old enough to understand what I'm saying. Will you open it now by yourself or shall we have to open it for you?

Not a move. Even her expression hadn't changed. Her breaths however were coming faster and faster. Then the battle began. I had to do it. I had to have a throat culture for her own protection. But first I told the parents that it was entirely up to them. I explained the danger but said that I would not insist on a throat examination so long as they would take the responsibility.

If you don't do what the doctor says you'll have to go to the hospital, the mother admonished her severely.

Oh yeah? I had to smile to myself. After all, I had already fallen in love with the savage brat, the parents were contemptible to me. In the ensuing struggle they grew more and more abject, crushed, exhausted while she surely rose to magnificent heights of insane fury of effort bred of her terror of me.

The father tried his best, and he was a big man but the fact that she was his daughter, his shame at her behavior and his dread of hurting her made him release her just at the critical moment several times when I had almost achieved success, till I wanted to kill him. But his dread also that she might have diphtheria made him tell me to go on, go on though he himself was almost fainting, while the mother moved back and forth behind us raising and lowering her hands in an agony of apprehension.

Put her in front of you on your lap, I ordered, and hold both her wrists.

But as soon as he did the child let out a scream. Don't, you're hurting me. Let go of my hands. Let them go I tell you. Then she shrieked terrifyingly, hysterically. Stop it! Stop it! You're killing me!

Do you think she can stand it, doctor! said the mother.

You get out, said the husband to his wife. Do you want her to die of diphtheria?

Come on now, hold her, I said.

Then I grasped the child's head with my left hand and tried to get the wooden tongue depressor between her teeth. She fought, with clenched teeth, desperately! But now I also had grown furious—at a child. I tried to hold myself down but I couldn't. I know how to expose a throat for inspection. And I did my best. When finally I got the wooden spatula behind the last teeth and just the point of it into the mouth cavity, she opened up for an instant but before I could see anything she came down again and gripping the wooden blade between her molars she reduced it to splinters before I could get it out again.

Aren't you ashamed, the mother yelled at her. Aren't you ashamed to act like that in front of the doctor?

Get me a smooth-handled spoon of some sort, I told the mother. We're going through with this. The child's mouth was already bleeding. Her tongue was cut and she was screaming in wild hysterical shrieks. Perhaps I should have desisted and come back in an hour or more. No doubt it would have been better. But I have seen at least two children lying dead in bed of neglect in such cases, and feeling that I must get a diagnosis now or never I went at it again. But the worst of it was that I too had got beyond reason. I could have torn the child apart in my own fury and enjoyed it. It was a pleasure to attack her. My face was burning with it.

The damned little brat must be protected against her own idiocy, one says to one's self at such times. Others must be protected against her. It is social necessity. And all these things are true. But a blind fury, a feeling of adult shame, bred of a longing for muscular release are the operatives. One goes on to the end.

In a final unreasoning assault I overpowered the child's neck and jaws. I forced the heavy silver spoon back of her teeth and down her throat till she gagged. And there it was—both tonsils covered with membrane. She had fought valiantly to keep me from knowing her secret. She had been hiding that sore throat for three days at least and lying to her parents in order to escape just such an outcome as this.

Now truly she *was* furious. She had been on the defensive before but now she attacked. Tried to get off her father's lap and fly at me while tears of defeat blinded her eyes.

An Interesting Social Study

Kristin Hunter

Cape May's newest summer resident settled herself as comfortably as possible in the strange stiff contours of a fanback wicker chair and awkwardly accepted a large tub-shaped glass of bourbon from her hostess.

But she was too conscious of too many things, including her wet bathing suit and bare feet, and the fine coating of sand which clung to them, to relax completely on Mrs. Powell's porch.

Noticing this, her hostess said, in her rich rumbling baritone, "You don't look a bit comfortable there." She stood up, an unusually tall and bony woman with a magnificently lined face which depicted, clearly as a graph, a mixed history of pleasure and pain.

"Here, try this rocking chair," she said in a tone less of invitation than command. "I'm sick and tired of rocking, anyway. That's all there is for an old woman like me to do in Cape May in the evenings. Sit on her porch, and rock, and get drunk."

"I always liked open porches in the summer," the new resident said. The rocking chair felt a little bit better. She began to sip the bourbon.

"Do you have a porch at your place?" Mrs. Powell's house guest inquired. She was a plump woman of vague shape and features, with wispy dyed-red hair; like her hostess, near sixty; and dressed, like her, for a city luncheon, in a silk suit, polished straw hat, and quantities of pearls. Except that Mrs. Powell's hair was uncompromisingly short and gray, and her pearls were real.

The new resident said, "Oh, no. I wish I did."

"Too bad," the house guest commiserated.

"Why on earth does she need a porch, Corinna?" Mrs. Powell inquired sharply. "She's not a housebound old relic like us." She drained her tub of bourbon. "She's young, and young people down here spend most of their time out of doors."

"Yes, but these big verandas *are* nice, especially in the evenings," the new resident half-sighed. Extensive galleries, some of them a block long, with pools of blue light reflected from their painted ceilings to inviting deck chairs; she had been eyeing them wistfully all through her after-beach walking tour of this incredible old town. Mrs. Powell's peremptory invitation, as she passed *her* veranda, to come up for a drink had been startling, invested with an almost-magical quality, like the instant fulfillment of a wish in childhood. Even now she could not quite believe it. She had met the older woman only yesterday, in the market, while shopping for groceries on her first day in Cape May.

"A big porch is nothing but a whole lot of extra work," Mrs. Powell declared, "especially when you have to keep it clean all by yourself. I've been down here a month now, and I still can't get a cleaning woman."

"You ought to talk to some of your colored boyfriends, Mrs. Powell," her house guest said playfully. "The trash man, or the garbage man. They might be able to get you somebody."

"Never you mind about my boyfriends, Corinna," Mrs. Powell answered in the same spirit. She turned to the new resident and said, "She's just jealous because I've kept my figure, and hers has gone to hell. I may be older than she is, but the men still turn and look at me, because I've still got a shape resembling a female's. I don't turn and look back at them, of course, because I'm only half a fool. Just enough fool to enjoy it."

She indicated her house guest and gave a rich, wicked chuckle. "Now, it wouldn't do for Corinna to have any kind of a shape left at her age, because she's one hundred per cent fool. If a man ever turned to look at her, even if he was only a trash man, she'd fall on him and faint for joy."

The new resident said nothing, but smiled. She was surprised by her amusement at this byplay, and also by the memories it aroused. It reminded her of nothing so much as the incessant joshing that had gone on for forty years between her grandmother, who sewed for wealthy ladies, and her seamstress-helper, a mountain of a woman named Pettina Brown.

"Don't pay Mrs. Powell any mind," the house guest said. "She's a fool. You heard her say so yourself."

"It's all right for me to say it, Corinna. But not for you." Mrs. Powell turned her intense, somber gaze on the younger woman. "Where are you staying while you're down here?"

"I have the Kinleys' cottage for the summer," the new resident said. "The little one over on Perry Street."

"I know which one it is," Mrs. Powell declared. "There's nothing in Cape May I *don't* know."

Including me, the new resident thought, staring resentfully but not without admiration at Mrs. Powell's bright restless eyes, like a large inquisitive bird's.–Before this evening is over, you'll know everything about *me*, too. That's probably why you invited me up here on your porch. You make it your business to know everything.

"The Kinleys," the house guest mused. "Aren't they those people from New York?" She answered her own question, "Yes, of course, that's who they are. I always wondered why they picked Cape May to spend their summers. It's a long way for them to travel for a little bit of ocean. Most of the people who own property around here come from nearer by. Baltimore and Delaware and the South."

"They come from all over now, Corinna," Mrs. Powell corrected, in her booming voice of authority. "Cape May is getting some new blood in it, thank God. It's about time–It's about time I sweetened your drink, too," she said, and poured two generous slugs of whiskey into the new resident's glass before she could say, "No, thank you."

"Well, I'm new here, but even I can see the town is changing," she heard herself say instead. "Some good changes, and some bad." It had been obvious today, for instance, that there was no longer any clear pattern of segregation on Cape May's beaches. A strong tide seemed to have scattered the varicolored bodies of bathers as randomly as shells. But last night she had noticed the stately old hotels floating at the edge of the water like giant ghost ships, empty, yet lit from stem to stern. They had given her an eerie feeling, and she had turned her back on the ocean wind and hurried home, shivering.

"I think it's a shame the way no one seems to go to the big hotels for dinner," she said. "They must have been popular once, but now everyone seems to be flocking to that ugly new nightclub down on the beach instead. The yellow one that looks like a mushroom."

"You have to consider Cape May as being two towns," Mrs. Powell explained. "The old summer people, and the new summer people. The old people are kind of wooden-headed and slow, and it takes them a long time to make up their minds about new things. But once they do make up their minds, they're set for life. The new people, now, they're like water, just flowing into any new open space that appears. Only, they don't stay anywhere very long. Just like water."

The new resident thought, And I'll bet you're the one who tells all the other old people what to think. I'll bet you run the whole town all by yourself, you old dragon.

"One thing, once the old people get to know you, there's not a thing they won't do for you," the house guest commented. "Southerners are like that. Hospitable."

"I think you're ready for another drink," Mrs. Powell announced, in that tone of a general giving incontrovertible orders.

The new resident said, with quick automatic politeness, "Oh, no. I've got to be going."

"Well, where in hell have you got to go?" Mrs. Powell demanded. "There's no place to go in Cape May."

"Well, maybe just half a drink, then."

Satisfied, Mrs. Powell nodded sharply, and snatched the glass away.

"You seem very young, child," the house guest commented while their hostess was gone. "Are you a student?"

"Yes," the new resident replied, "and thanks, but I'm not *that* young. I finished college eight years ago. Last year I went back to graduate school."

"It's so hard to get in a good school these days," the house guest complained. "When I was a young girl, it was easy. I went to *two* good schools, one right after the other. I went to Finch, and before that I went to the National Cathedral School, in Washington, D.C."

"If you went to all those schools, how come you're still so dumb, Corinna?" Mrs. Powell demanded, returning with a bottle from which she poured two brimming tubs of bourbon for her guests.

The house guest accepted the bourbon as good-naturedly as she accepted Mrs. Powell's tyranny, as if both were divinely ordained circumstances, and replied, "When I was growing up, girls weren't supposed to train for careers. We went to school to become young ladies. Those schools I went to, National Cathedral and Finch, were mostly finishing schools."

"Well, this one's a young lady, and she's smart, besides." Mrs.

Powell turned her fierce dark gaze on the new resident. "Not that anybody gives a damn around here, but where did you attend school?"

"Spelman College, in Atlanta."

The house guest reflected a moment. "I don't believe I've heard of that one. Is that a finishing school for girls?"

The new resident paused, then said in a somewhat surprised tone, "Well, yes it is, actually. It's funny, I never thought of it that way, but actually, that's what it is."

"Well, I think a finishing school education is still the best sort for a young girl. At National Cathedral, we had teas every Friday afternoon for the faculty and our guests."

"So did we, at Spelman," the new resident said eagerly. "Funny, I had forgotten all about those faculty teas. All the girls were so anxious to get away for the weekend, we hated staying around for them, but really, they were kind of nice. Everybody got all dressed up, and in good weather we were served out of doors, on a big porch."

"Well, I don't think they teach you a damn thing at those young-lady schools, especially in the South," Mrs. Powell declared. "I went to Spence, myself. And I was never allowed south of the Plaza." She elevated a stupendous column of wrinkled, warted, hairy throat, like a camel's, and laughed outrageously, adding, "I was a *brilliant* student."

The house guest winked. "Mrs. Powell means she just barely got through with passing grades. That was brilliant for *her*."

"Oh, Corinna, hush," Mrs. Powell said amiably. "Your large mouth just indicates to everybody how small your brain really is."

It was that hour in Cape May, between seven and eight in the evening, when the light turns lavender and liquid and the huge Mississippi-steamboat houses, each with two or more tiers of balconies, seem about to cast off in it and float downstream. The air was also heavy with honeysuckle, and the new resident, two days away from the city, yawned deliciously, then caught herself and returned to her stiff posture, as if she had no right to relax. "I just love these big old houses," she said.

"Well most of them are so old and run-down they're falling apart," Mrs. Powell said. "You should've seen this old wreck when I first bought it. Looked like a nigra house that hadn't been painted in forty years."

In the strangely colored twilight that falls on the southernmost point on the Jersey shore, the new resident's hands, as they caught the arms of the rocker, were tinted a soft mauve, while the faces of the older women, who had already spent a month in the sun, were deeper variations of the same shade.

"Where did you say you're attending school now?" the house guest inquired.

"Bryn Mawr, in Pennsylvania," the new resident said. She spoke now in clipped, factual phrases. "For a master's degree. In social work."

"Well, we could use some social workers down here," Mrs. Powell said. "Cape May is full of fretful old people, all useless and mostly alcoholics."

The new resident said softly, almost to herself, "I wanted a quiet place to work on my thesis this summer. That's why I picked Cape May. Besides, I heard it was a pretty town."

"Well, you came to the right place if you wanted quiet," Mrs. Powell said, pouring herself another double slug of whiskey. "This town is so damn quiet it gets on my nerves sometimes."

"Oh, no more, please, thank you," the new resident said, too late.

"If you like pretty things," the house guest said between sips, "you ought to get Mrs. Powell to show you the inside of her house. It's the prettiest house in Cape May."

"It is not," Mrs. Powell said firmly. "It's just a huge, old run-down wreck. Like me."

"Bryn Mawr's a good school, I hear," the house guest said in her weak, but penetrating voice, with a register like a piccolo's. "It's so hard to get into a good school these days. My grandson had to apply to seven schools before he got accepted into one. Princeton was one that turned him down. The other day I met a boy who had gotten accepted into Princeton, and I looked at him and said, 'Just stand still a minute and let me touch you. You're so smart, I want some of your brains to rub off on me.' "

Mrs. Powell laughed raucously. "Well, it didn't work that time, Corinna. You're still dumb as hell. But you're lucky. You've got another chance. Here's another smart one sitting right here. Why don't you touch her?"

She offered the bottle to the new resident, who shook her head.

"The damn thing's empty, anyway," Mrs. Powell observed. "I have a reserve supply in the house, though. Even if you won't have another drink, at least come inside and see my old run-down house. It's the worst wreck in Cape May, so you might find it an interesting social study."

This invitation, or command, was accompanied by a powerful tug on the young woman's hand by the other's gnarled and splendidly jeweled one.

–All right, the new resident thought, let's get it over with. I didn't come here looking to be accepted, anyway. She took a deep breath and said, "Thank you. I will."

"Welcome to my hovel," Mrs. Powell said. "Fixing it up almost broke my back, and it's still a mess. But I love it."

She flicked on an overpowering chandelier, illuminating a thirty-foot dining room with the cool, unreal beauty of an undersea cave. White curtains billowed at its tall French windows, and pale green paint had made its quantities of massive old furniture seem floating and fragile. The only ornaments were a portrait over the sideboard and, on the long, frosty-green dining table, a centerpiece of tall green candles in silver holders and bunches of real green grapes.

"Lovely," the new resident said, and caught her breath again as Mrs. Powell's enormous diamonds flashed in the light from the chandelier.

"Oh, it needs a lot more work," Mrs. Powell said, with a deprecating wave of hands like blazing claws. "But I'm too old and tired to be bothered with it any more. One of my guests said to me the other day, 'Mrs. Powell, there isn't a thing in this house to let a person know they're at the seashore. Couldn't you at least add a few seashells to that damn centerpiece?' And I told her, 'Yes, I know, it's a good idea, but by the time I've finished breaking my back cleaning around here, I'm too tired to go down to the beach and lug back any God damn shells. I'm too tired, and I'm too damn old.'–Now, if you'll excuse me, I'm going back in the kitchen for another drink. I'm the biggest lush in Cape May, but I'm so old it doesn't matter to anybody. I *love* old age."

The new resident moved closer to the long carved grape-green sideboard to study the portrait that hung above it, of a tall, gaunt man with the same deep, restless, ultimately somber eyes as Mrs. Powell's.

"That's Mrs. Powell's daddy there," the house guest piped. "I'll bet you don't know who he was. For a number of years he was the United States Senator from North Carolina." Her voice grew more shrill. "Mrs. Powell is just about the most important lady in Cape May."

"Corinna, hush," Mrs. Powell said sternly, returning with a bottle and an ice bucket and the three titanic glasses on a tray. "If there's anything I can't stand, it's big-mouthed people who go bragging about you to other people."

"Well, how would people know anything about you if other people didn't tell them, Mrs. Powell?" the house guest inquired, with shrill logic. "She's a student, she's interested in history. I thought she might like to know about your father."

"Well, maybe she's interested in history, and maybe she isn't, Corinna," Mrs. Powell rebuked her. "Here, don't stand on politeness. Help yourselves to a little nightcap."

The room seemed suddenly full of fireworks, exploding from the brilliant chandelier to the diamonds on Mrs. Powell's hands to the ice cubes she was handling with flashing silver tongs.

"Cheers," Mrs. Powell said, gulping her drink and patting her stomach. "Ah. Nothing goes down like good old country bourbon.– I'll tell her one thing about my family, though, if she's interested in history. She may not like it, but I'll tell her this one thing anyway, and maybe she'll find it interesting." She set her glass down on the sideboard and assumed a graceless stance, chin elevated and feet widely separated, like some defiant, battered colossus. "My great-grandfather was the biggest slaveholder in our state. He had over nine hundred slaves." She stared unblinking at the new resident. "I hope you don't mind hearing a thing like that about my family." Holding the pose, she looked monumental and splendid as the old beach-front hotels, and as lonely.

"Not at all," the new resident said. She set her drink back on the tray without tasting it. "I have to run home now, though."

"What's your hurry?" the house guest asked. "Finish your drink. It's only eight o'clock."

"Now, Corinna," Mrs. Powell said without moving, "let her go if she wants to. That way she won't be afraid to come back here again."

"I should have changed out of this wet bathing suit hours ago," the new resident said. She paused carefully, waiting to find out what else she wanted to say. When she knew, it surprised her, as had nearly all of her reactions on this odd evening.

"Besides," she went on, "I picked up a lot of lovely shells on the beach yesterday. It was my first day on the beach, and I was so greedy, I took home more than I can keep. I want to bring some of them back here, so Mrs. Powell can pick out the ones she likes best, for her centerpiece. That is, if she would like me to."

Mrs. Powell still held the pose, like an old edifice too proud to yield to its awful, imminent tendency to crumble.

The new resident moved quickly to the door and said, "Well, good night. Thank you for an interesting time." She was halfway outside when Mrs. Powell found her voice, a faltering croak that soon expanded to its normal bass-tuba resonance.

"Well, come back when you can," she said. "I have a lot of interesting old relics around here, if you like history, and I'm the biggest old relic of them all. Although I don't care much for history, myself."

The Loves of Franklin Ambrose

Joyce Carol Oates

A decade before the phrase "Black is beautiful" became popular, Franklin Ambrose knew that he was beautiful. But his beauty had nothing to do with being black. He was naturally handsome in a small, neat way; he cultivated a thin mustache and a very black, rugged, almost savage goatee; his shoes were so shiny that they looked varnished; he wore Pierre Cardin shirts of various peacock-gay colors, expensive silk-twill ties and ascots, and suits whose notched and peaked lapels expanded and narrowed according to fashion laws totally unknown to Frank's mundane, hard-working colleagues at the university. He took an obvious, healthy pride in physical appearances and was critical of his wife's clothes, which always seemed shapeless and dowdy. "Do you want to embarrass me?" he sometimes asked in exasperation.

But most of the time he was cheerful and very energetic. He hastened to put all white people at their ease, immediately, by emphasizing the scorn he felt for anything "black" (he hated that modish word; he preferred the more sanitary and middle-class "Negro"). In fact, he accepted a position at a small university in southern Canada, near Hamilton, because he suspected—correctly—that there would be few Negroes in the school. He had only one real rival—a popular professor of psychology who sported an Afro haircut and love beads; but Franklin put him down by saying, whenever the man's name was mentioned, "There's a real professional black." This made his white friends laugh appreciatively.

Franklin was not "black," but he was very professional. His

degrees were all from Harvard and he had spent a year in England as a Fulbright Fellow; during that time, he had developed a faint, clipped English accent. At Harvard he had been very popular with Radcliffe girls, especially a kind of bright, intense Jewish girl who shared many of his interests in literature and music. But he wanted to marry another kind of girl—he didn't know why, exactly—he had his heart set on a Wellesley girl whose father was a judge in Boston, a sweet girl, not very intelligent but gifted with a pale, smooth, almost porcelain complexion. Their marriage was violently opposed by her family, but Franklin won, and in 1965 he accepted a position at Hilberry University and took his bride to a small city in southeastern Ontario: with great anticipation, a sense of drama, for he was the only Negro in the English department and the only Harvard man.

Frank became the department's most popular professor at once. And yet something began to happen in the second year: He felt a strange, aimless melancholy, his classroom successes came too easily, he noticed that he and Eunice, out together, no longer attracted the attention and the occasional outraged glares they had attracted in the past. No doubt about it, Eunice was becoming dowdy, her waist and hips thickening; she was not even very pretty. The only happiness in Frank's life was his twin sons, wonderfully light, almost fair little boys, with beautiful features—especially their dark, thickly lashed eyes. At times he stared at them as if unable to believe the miracle of their physical beauty. How had anything so wonderful happened to him?

As his wife's looks dwindled and Frank began to sink into the ordinary routine of teaching in an ordinary university—no overwrought, neurotic, brilliant Radcliffe girls to stir the adrenaline!—he felt at times a sense of panic. What, he was 28 years old? What, already he was 30? For his 32nd birthday he gifted himself with a white MG, though his family could obviously not fit in it. He bought an elegant, rather Beau Brummellish smoking jacket to wear in his study at home and a sueded-calfskin belted coat that drew all eyes to it as he strolled across the gray-lit campus. He began going with his students to The Cave, a popular pub, crowded and noisy and merry; the majority of his student friends were boys, who eagerly appreciated his wit and his friendliness—most of the other professors nervously avoided all personal contact with students—but a few were girls. They were all the same type, more or less: intellectual, casual, a little brazen, a little sloppy, and they seemed to appreciate

Frank even more than the boys did.

A possibility dawned on Frank.

Yes, he was attracted to the girls as if to searing, caressing rays of light: their pale skins, their moving, twisting, smirking, giggling mouths, their tight, thigh-high skirts, their nervous writhing mannerisms when they came in for "conferences" to his office. They brushed their long hair out of their eyes and smiled at him. Frank would feel at such times an intoxication that forced him to lean forward, gazing at them, his own eyes bright and his flesh livened by their closeness. They complained to him about their families or their other professors or their boyfriends: "My boyfriend is, I don't know, he's so *dumb* compared with someone like you, Dr. Ambrose. . . . I mean, he's so *dumb* when it comes to conversation that I just sort of blank out and think about, well, you, I guess. I mean I think about how funny you were in class or something and . . . well . . . I think about *you* when I'm with him, you know, when the two of us are . . . you know . . . I feel real rotten about it, because it isn't fair, I guess, to him, because we're really sort of in love . . . and . . . and . . . " And they would gaze at Frank with their eyes sometimes misting over. At such times he felt his heart beat with certainty: *Unmistakable!*

The girls were so sweet, with their kisses and their sudden, rationed tears, that Frank went about in a perpetual daze, more genial than ever before.

Being a gentleman, he made no more than the most subtle of allusions to his colleagues in the department, most of whom were prematurely weary, slowed down with families, balding, thickening, and yet still fired feebly with hopes of romance; they were temporarily freshened by stray rumors of secret liaisons, even though the liaisons never happened to them. They appreciated Frank, who was, after all, black (the word began to be used, cautiously, around 1969–1970), so trim and handsome and elegantly turned out, and they quipped that he was their liaison man with the students.

"Frank will bridge the generation gap for us," they said with wistful, encouraging smiles.

But then, in the late Sixties, an essay with the title "The Student as Nigger" became widely circulated; it was even published in the student newspaper. Frank was aghast. He couldn't believe it. Colleagues and students began talking quite familiarly, openly, of the oppression of students and "niggers"—often in Frank's presence, as if to demonstrate to him how liberal and understanding they were. *The word nigger! On everyone's lips!* Frank was furious, demoralized, befuddled; he would not explain his moods to his wife; he went out one evening by himself to a cocktail lounge far from the university, where he got drunk and had to be sent home in a taxicab. At such times, when he was very drunk, he had the confused idea that some white man—any white man at all—was trying to appropriate his twin boys. "They want to take my babies away, my babies," he would weep. "They want to take my babies because I'm black and my babies are white. . . ."

He knew he was not a nigger, and yet he wasn't sure that other people, glancing at him, knew. He recalled with horror the evening, at a faculty party, when the slightly drunken wife of a colleague had cornered him to ask whether he planned "to go back to the ghetto to help his people," seeing that he himself was so successful. That white bitch!

But his young girl students fawned over him, even pursued him, singly and in small packs. There was no doubt of his manhood with *them.* Their names were Cindy and Laurie and Sandy and Cheryl; they passed in and out of his arms with the rotation of the academic semesters, some of them wise and cynical with experience, others incredibly naive and therefore dangerous; they were like figures in the most riotous, improbable of his adolescent dreams, somehow lacking substance, lacking souls, because of their very eagerness to oblige him. "But, Dr. Ambrose, you're a genius from Harvard and all that, I'm afraid to talk to you, I'm afraid you're giving me a grade when you just *look* at me!" One of the Cindys or Sandys whose bold stare had misled Frank nearly caused a scandal by confessing to her parents, who in turn called the university's president and several members of the board of trustees; but after a four-hour conference in the president's office, Franklin managed to be forgiven. He promised not to be "indiscreet" again.

That was in the winter of 1969. In the spring of that year, the appointments and promotions committee (called the hiring and firing committee) of the department interviewed applicants for the position of lecturer in English. Franklin was the youngest member of this powerful committee and he grilled candidates for the job seriously. He was not very impressed with a young Ph.D. from Yale nor with a young Indian student from Oxford; he was very impressed with a young woman named Molly Holt, who rushed in 15 minutes late for her interview, wearing a very short leather skirt and bright-gold boots.

Franklin stared at this girl. She was no more than five feet, one or two, and therefore shorter than he. She was very pretty, with a small, pixylike face, blonde hair snipped short and puffed out carelessly about her face, so young, so pretty, with impressive recommendations from the University of Chicago! It was hard to believe. Frank's interest in her grew as he glanced through her application and saw that she was a divorcee with a three-year-old son. She was answering questions pertly and brightly. Obviously an intelligent woman. Frank was careful to ask her questions that might lead her to admirable statements: "I am deeply committed to literature and to teaching, yes," she said. "And to the future, to the struggle for equality between men and women." Hastily, Frank asked her about her doctoral thesis, which she had just begun: "It's called *Crises of Sexual Identity in Trollope and Dickens,"* she said. "It grew out of my fascination with the role of women in Victorian literature. Imagine, Charles Dickens created Edith Dombey!—and yet in his personal life he was such a bastard, a real male chauvinist pig—"

After this, it took Frank several hours and several meetings of the committee to hire Miss Holt: He had a lot of talking to do.

When she arrived in September, he drove her around in his neat little white sports car, helping her locate an apartment, helping her unpack books (she had a small mountain of books); he lent himself out as her escort at university functions for the first few weeks. Someone sent his wife an anonymous note that said, "Your husband is extremely attentive to a certain young lady professor," but Frank tore it up with such contempt and such finesse that his wife could not help but believe him, though she wept. Frank, in Molly Holt's company, was careful to be polite and witty and distant, never staring too boldly at her nor taking up her vivacious comments—she was always complimenting him on his clothes—as if he feared what might happen might happen too quickly. Molly herself dressed rather flamboyantly for a young lady with her rigorous academic background (before Chicago, she had gone to Bennington); she was always hurrying through the department's corridors in miniskirts and serapes and boots and then, as the fashions gradually changed, in pants and a blouse that clung tightly to her firm, intense little body. At department meetings she was a little arch; she sometimes interrupted people, even the head of the department, a small white-haired man named Barth. "We must all learn to be more *contemporary,"* she urged.

Frank had lunch with her every day, hung around her office, drove her to her apartment in bad weather, talked her into joining him and his students at The Cave. But she was always anxious to get home, to relieve her baby sitter and to work on her classroom preparations; she was so serious! At times Frank's patient grin began to ache, waiting for her to get through with all this seriousness and talk of literature and "relevance." They sat crowded together in pub booths, arguing and complimenting each other; from time to time a sharp, almost searing glance flashed between them and Frank would feel a little dizzy with certainty. . . . But always she had to get home, always she was gathering up her big leather purse and striding away, and he would be left with his gaggle of students.

At home, he sat in his study, in his big black-leather chair, and thought about Molly. His wife's comfortable, bovine presence annoyed him; even his boys distracted him from his dreams of Molly. Sometimes he went out late at night, saying he needed cigarettes (he had begun smoking again, after meeting Molly, breaking his five-year period of abstinence); he telephoned Molly to ask how she was. She always said, "Very busy! My head is whirling, I have so much to do! But I love it." Frank could not decide if she were being deliberately coy. She really confused him. So he would ask if she needed any help, if she needed a mature, male viewpoint . . . he would be glad to drop in . . . .

But she always said, "No, thanks! It's very thoughtful of you, though."

As the winter deepened and the Ontario sky became perpetually smudged, pressing low upon the spirit, even Molly began to slow down. Frank noticed that her stride was not quite so energetic, and one of his colleagues commented zestfully: "It looks like Molly is coming in for a landing, like the rest of us." Frank took her out for coffee and asked her if anything was wrong. She wore an outfit that seemed to be made of green burlap, hanging dramatically about her and highlighting her small, serious face.

"Well, I've been working very hard this semester," she said slowly. "I have so many student compositions to correct. I'm way behind on my dissertation."

"Anything else?"

Molly hesitated. "Well, I'm having trouble with my ex-husband. He's trying to get out of the child-support payments. He is such a bastard, you wouldn't know. Or, yes, maybe you would know," she said, raising her eyes dramatically to Frank.

They were sitting in a small, grimy coffee shop; Frank dared public attention and patted her hand. It was a very small, delicate, pale hand, and the sight of his own dark hand on it pleased him, excited him. *Unmistakable!*

"Maybe I would know, yes," he said, wondering what he meant by this.

"You and I understand each other. We have so much in common, so much . . ." Molly said, her large brown eyes filling with tears. "Oh, sometimes I could scream, this whole university is filled with fossils who don't *understand,* they just don't *understand.*"

And then, as if she'd confessed too much, she hurried away to a class. Frank was left sitting there, stunned, wondering if he were falling in love.

Obviously, he had never been in love before.

She avoided him for several days after this; he asked her to lunch and their conversation was interrupted by the intrusion of the department's would-be poet, Ron Blazack; Frank called her one evening when his wife was at a meeting of the Faculty Wives' Association, told her he had something to say to her and talked her into letting him come over.

"All right," she said reluctantly, "but give me time to put Jimmy to bed . . . he hasn't been feeling well."

When he got there, he was a little disappointed at the way her apartment was furnished. "I'm trying to live within my means," she said dryly. She offered him a drink, though, and Frank smiled happily. He believed he could feel how dazzling his smile was.

"Let's talk," he said. "Are you happy here?"

"Yes. No. Not really," she said.

Such a pretty young woman, in spite of the circles of fatigue under her eyes! She wore black net stockings with a diamond design that made Frank lose track of the conversation now and then. She was complaining about her ex-husband and then about the heavy teaching load. "But, Frank, this job means more to me than anything right now. Thank God you people hired me! So many universities turned me down . . . I was getting desperate. My son has this allergy problem I told you about, and I don't have medical coverage for him, and I was really getting panicked. I think that some English departments wouldn't hire me because of my appearance, maybe, or my views on things," she said, looking Frank in the eye, as if he might not believe so bizarre a statement. Frank nodded slowly. "And of course there's the male chauvinism to fight. God, what a fight it's going to be! Centuries of discrimination and prejudice. Men have got to be re-educated if it destroys them."

She stared down at her polished nails and her several big, metallic rings. Frank wondered why she had referred to men as "them" in his presence, as if she weren't talking to a man. This was strange.

"Have men exploited you very much?" Frank asked.

"God, yes."

He got up and went to sit beside her. She laughed bitterly.

"Why don't you tell me about it?" he said in a gentle voice.

"Thank you, but I'm not a self-pitying woman. Thank you anyway," she said, drawing back from him. "But you know what it's like."

"What it's like?"

"To be discriminated against."

Frank stared at her.

"What's wrong?" she said.

Frank began to stammer. "Just what–what did you mean by that statement? Would you kindly explain that statement?"

"What statement?"

"That I–I'm supposed to know–supposed to know what it's like to be discriminated against—"

"Well, don't you?" Molly asked. "Being a black, you've been treated like dirt by the white male establishment–haven't you? Haven't they victimized you? Blacks and women are both—"

Frank could not believe his ears. He grabbed her arm.

"Well, we didn't get together tonight to talk about that kind of stuff," he said hotly; and as she tugged away from him, he felt his accent slipping, growing richer, thicker, "there's anything I hate, it's a woman who talks too much—"

"What? You're crazy!"

"*You're* crazy!" Frank yelled. A flame seemed to burn in his brain, he was so angry. "Look, you been givin' me the eye now for four months an' I been tailin' around after you as if I got nothin' better to do, when Jesus Christ, there are little girls waitin' in line–*I mean waitin' in line,* sister–so don't hand me none of this crap—"

Molly jumped to her feet. She yanked his pale-yellow ascot out of his shirt and up onto his face, so that he was blinded for a second.

"Get the hell out of here! Go home, to your honkie wife!" she cried.

He went home, furious. He was never to speak to her again.

For weeks he went around muttering to himself, avoiding Molly in the hall, avoiding even his students. When a red-haired freshman dropped in to chat with him about the "erotic symbolism of T. S. Eliot," he did not trust his assessment of her sweet little smiles. No, he couldn't trust his judgment. Was the girl really smiling so deeply at him? Or was he being fooled again?

One day Frank put on his neatest, grayest suit, asked the head of the department, Dr. Barth, to call an emergency meeting of the appointments and promotions committee, and explained in a terse, quiet voice that his "special relationship" with the student body allowed him to know things that the rest of the department did not know.

When the meeting was convened, Frank spoke first. "The students have no respect for Miss Holt," he said sadly. "They laugh at her—evidently, she mispronounces words. She doesn't prepare her lectures. I've overheard her talking with students in the coffee shop and she actually gives them misinformation—it's just pathetic, unbelievable. I've put off telling you this, because the situation is so ugly. But it was on my strong recommendation that she was hired last year and it's my responsibility now to tell you what is going on."

"No complaints about her have come to me," Dr. Barth said slowly.

"The students are reluctant to talk to you, Dr. Barth," Frank said, "because you're—well, you're so obviously above their trivial problems, so they think. They come to me because there's—well, I suppose less of an age difference."

Dr. Barth nodded gravely. "Yes, I know I'm out of touch with this generation. I know. But about Miss Holt: There may be trouble dismissing her. She's going to be awarded a Ph.D. from Chicago, after all."

"No, she hasn't been working on her dissertation all year," Frank said. "I don't know what she's been doing. Actually, I wonder about her professional commitment."

The other members of the committee murmured agreement.

Frank went on solemnly. "It comes down to the preservation of our professional standards. We cannot afford," he said, looking from face to face, "in this time of disintegrating values, to have so casual and uncommitted a teacher in our department. Miss Holt is just not respected by her students. Evidently, she refers to the rest of us, in her classes, as *fossils*."

"Fossils?"

"I told you it was an ugly situation," Frank said softly.

Dr. Barth called a special meeting of the entire department for Monday morning. Molly came in late and Frank did no more than glance at her, nervously. She pulled out a chair at the far end of the big oval table everyone was seated around and the giddiness of her outfit—really, she had gone too far, wearing a loose-knit black tunic over violet-jersey pants to school!—seemed to show everyone how hopeless she was. Dr. Barth began the meeting in his usual grim, paternal voice, his hands clasped in front of him. He spoke of unpleasant reports, of an unfortunate situation, of the rigorous standards of this particular department, etc., etc. He was the only one who was looking at Molly, who in her turn was glancing around, curiously. Frank stared at his own manicured fingernails. His heart raced. Why, the old man sounded so sorry for her, was he going to change his mind? Maybe just reprimand her?

Dr. Barth said, "Because of special circumstances, the committee on appointments and promotions has been forced to suggest that the contract of Miss Holt not be renewed for next year. This decision was reached after many hours of anguish, after many, many hours of discussion. There are budget problems, also, which might involve our slightly reducing the salaries of other department members, unless the lectureship held by Miss Holt is terminated. But this should in no way, of course, influence your vote on the matter. Under the terms of our bylaws, I have therefore called this meeting of the department to request that you support the committee's recommendation and terminate Miss Holt's contract."

Molly was gaping at him.

"What?" she said faintly.

No one dared look at her. Many of the department members had been told by Dr. Barth of the reason for the meeting; the others stared at one another in disbelief.

Molly, sitting so pertly at the far end of the table, seemed suddenly to shrink.

"But why? What are the reasons? Can't I defend myself?"

"Under the terms of our university bylaws," Dr. Barth said gently, "no reasons for nonrenewal of contract need be stated. Only in the case of nonrenewal of a tenured faculty member need reasons be given."

"But I . . . I don't understand. . . ."

Frank glanced down at her. That small, pale face! That white bitch!

"If you would like to say anything, I'm sure we would all listen with sympathy," Dr. Barth said.

"I . . . I. . . ."

She fell silent.

After a minute or so, Dr. Barth said, "Then we really should get on with the vote. Some of us have eleven-o'clock classes we must teach."

Stiff white slips of paper were passed around for the vote.

Frank scribbled "Dismissal" on his ballot at once, folded it neatly in two and then in two again.

Next to him sat old Miss Snyder, a back number from the university's really mediocre years; with her billowing gray dresses and her stern, medieval nose, she had always disliked Molly Holt. No problem there. On Frank's left was the poet, Blazack, who kept shifting miserably in his seat. Around the large, highly polished table everyone sat in silence, staring down at their ballots. They seemed reluctant to vote. The only people who sat with their heads up were Frank and Dr. Barth and Molly, whose ballot lay before her, untouched.

"Really, we must hurry. It's a quarter to eleven," Dr. Barth said.

The ballots were collected by the departmental secretary and counted out. Frank could overhear the count: *For* dismissal. *Against* dismissal. He began to sweat, wondering if he might lose. What if . . . ? What if . . . ? What if that bitch had managed to win her way into the hearts of the other professors? What if she'd told them the same hard-luck story she had told him? What if they refused to believe him? His nostrils flared. In that case, he would quit. Would quit. Would quit with dignity. Yes, he would quit. He would not remain in this department if his professional integrity were doubted.

Dr. Barth announced the results: "The vote is sixteen to five for nonrenewal of Miss Holt's contract."

Molly pushed her chair back clumsily and got to her feet. "But I . . . I still don't understand. . . ."

"I will be happy to talk with you and to make suggestions about where you might apply for a new position," Dr. Barth said at once. "In fact, we would all be happy to help you."

Molly snatched up her big leather purse and hurried out of the room.

Relief.

Frank lingered with some of the others, shaking his head gravely as they shook theirs. He had to admit he'd been taken in by her . . . he had to admit he'd made a mistake. . . . The whole ugly mess was his fault, he said.

"No, don't blame yourself, Frank," everyone said.

Dr. Barth patted his arm. "Frank, we belong to a profession with extremely rigorous standards. Personal feelings shouldn't enter into it at all. I'm sure Miss Holt will be happier in another university, with less demanding criteria of excellence."

But Frank found it difficult to be comforted. He felt really down. Instead of going out to The Cave with his students that afternoon, he went right home. His wife was frightened by his dour, peevish frown.

"You're not sick, Frank?"

No, not sick. He put on his smoking jacket and went to sit in his leather chair; he wanted to be alone. His wife opened his study door to ask, meekly, if he wanted dinner delayed. "Yes. Maybe an hour," he said. She then asked if the twins could come play with him for a few minutes—they'd been waiting for him to come home all day.

Frank considered this.

His eyes traveled up from his excellent shoes to his slim, checked trousers, to the casual richness of his navy-blue smoking jacket. He had knotted a white ascot quickly around his neck. He sensed his totality, his completion—a man who did not need anyone else, certainly not a woman. But he had lived through a certain emotional experience—there was no doubt in his mind that it had been an experience—and though he had triumphed, still he felt a little melancholy. It was a delicate, sensitive melancholy and the twins were so healthy and noisy that they might destroy it.

Finally, he said, "No, not right now. I want to be alone. I feel a little melancholy and I want to be alone."

Counterparts

James Joyce

The bell rang furiously and, when Miss Parker went to the tube, a furious voice called out in a piercing North of Ireland accent:

"Send Farrington here!"

Miss Parker returned to her machine, saying to a man who was writing at a desk:

"Mr. Alleyne wants you upstairs."

The man muttered "*Blast* him!" under his breath and pushed back his chair to stand up. When he stood up he was tall and of great bulk. He had a hanging face, dark wine-coloured, with fair eyebrows and moustache: his eyes bulged forward slightly and the whites of them were dirty. He lifted up the counter and, passing by the clients, went out of the office with a heavy step.

He went heavily upstairs until he came to the second landing, where a door bore a brass plate with the inscription *Mr. Alleyne.* Here he halted, puffing with labour and vexation, and knocked. The shrill voice cried:

"Come in!"

The man entered Mr. Alleyne's room. Simultaneously Mr. Alleyne, a little man wearing goldrimmed glasses on a clean-shaven face, shot his head up over a pile of documents. The head itself was so pink and hairless it seemed like a large egg reposing on the papers. Mr. Alleyne did not lose a moment:

"Farrington? What is the meaning of this? Why have I always to complain of you? May I ask you why you haven't made a copy of that contract between Bodley and Kirwan? I told you it must be ready by four o'clock."

"But Mr. Shelley said, sir—"

"Mr. Shelley said, sir. . . . Kindly attend to what I say and not to what *Mr. Shelley says, sir.* You have always some excuse or another for shirking work. Let me tell you that if the contract is not copied before this evening I'll lay the matter before Mr. Crosbie. . . . Do you hear me now?"

"Yes, sir."

"Do you hear me now? . . . Ay and another little matter! I might as well be talking to the wall as talking to you. Understand once for all that you get a half an hour for your lunch and not an hour and a half. How many courses do you want, I'd like to know. . . . Do you mind me now?"

"Yes, sir."

Mr. Alleyne bent his head again upon his pile of papers. The man stared fixedly at the polished skull which directed the affairs of Crosbie & Alleyne, gauging its fragility. A spasm of rage gripped his throat for a few moments and then passed, leaving after it a sharp sensation of thirst. The man recognised the sensation and felt that he must have a good night's drinking. The middle of the month was passed and, if he could get the copy done in time, Mr. Alleyne might give him an order on the cashier. He stood still, gazing fixedly at the head upon the pile of papers. Suddenly Mr. Alleyne began to upset all the papers, searching for something. Then, as if he had been unaware of the man's presence till that moment, he shot up his head again, saying:

"Eh? Are you going to stand there all day? Upon my word, Farrington, you take things easy!"

"I was waiting to see . . ."

"Very good, you needn't wait to see. Go downstairs and do your work."

The man walked heavily towards the door and, as he went out of the room, he heard Mr. Alleyne cry after him that if the contract was not copied by evening Mr. Crosbie would hear of the matter.

He returned to his desk in the lower office and counted the sheets which remained to be copied. He took up his pen and dipped it in the ink but he continued to stare stupidly at the last words he had written: *In no case shall the said Bernard Bodley be* . . . The evening was falling and in a few minutes they would be lighting the gas: then he could write. He felt that he must slake the thirst in his throat. He stood up from his desk and, lifting the counter as before, passed out of the office. As he was passing out the chief clerk looked at him inquiringly.

"It's all right, Mr. Shelley," said the man, pointing with his finger to indicate the objective of his journey.

The chief clerk glanced at the hat-rack, but, seeing the row complete, offered no remark. As soon as he was on the landing the man pulled a shepherd's plaid cap out of his pocket, put it on his head and ran quickly down the rickety stairs. From the street door he walked on furtively on the inner side of the path towards the corner and all at once dived into a doorway. He was now safe in the dark snug of O'Neill's shop, and, filling up the little window that looked into the bar with his inflamed face, the colour of dark wine or dark meat, he called out:

"Here, Pat, give us a g.p., like a good fellow."

The curate brought him a glass of plain porter. The man drank it at a gulp and asked for a caraway seed. He put his penny on the counter and, leaving the curate to grope for it in the gloom, retreated out of the snug as furtively as he had entered it.

Darkness, accompanied by a thick fog, was gaining upon the dusk of February and the lamps in Eustace Street had been lit. The man went up by the houses until he reached the door of the office, wondering whether he could finish his copy in time. On the stairs a moist pungent odour of perfumes saluted his nose: evidently Miss Delacour had come while he was out in O'Neill's. He crammed his cap back again into his pocket and re-entered the office, assuming an air of absent-mindedness.

"Mr. Alleyne has been calling for you," said the chief clerk severely. "Where were you?"

The man glanced at the two clients who were standing at the counter as if to intimate that their presence prevented him from answering. As the clients were both male the chief clerk allowed himself a laugh.

"I know that game," he said. "Five times in one day is a little bit. . . . Well, you better look sharp and get a copy of our correspondence in the Delacour case for Mr. Alleyne."

This address in the presence of the public, his run upstairs and the porter he had gulped down so hastily confused the man and, as he sat down at his desk to get what was required, he realised how hopeless was the task of finishing his copy of the contract before half past five. The dark damp night was coming and he longed to spend it in the bars, drinking with his friends amid the glare of gas and the clatter of glasses. He got out the Delacour correspondence and passed out of the office. He hoped Mr. Alleyne would not discover that the last two letters were missing.

The moist pungent perfume lay all the way up to Mr. Alleyne's room. Miss Delacour was a middle-aged woman of Jewish appearance. Mr. Alleyne was said to be sweet on her or on her money. She came to the office often and stayed a long time when she came. She was sitting beside his desk now in an aroma of perfumes, smoothing the handle of her umbrella and nodding the great black feather in her hat. Mr. Alleyne had swivelled his chair round to face her and thrown his right foot jauntily upon his left knee. The man put the correspondence on the desk and bowed respectfully but neither Mr. Alleyne nor Miss Delacour took any notice of his bow. Mr. Alleyne tapped a finger on the correspondence and then flicked it towards him as if to say: *"That's all right: you can go."*

The man returned to the lower office and sat down again at his desk. He stared intently at the incomplete phrase: *In no case shall the said Bernard Bodley be* . . . and thought how strange it was that the last three words began with the same letter. The chief clerk began to hurry Miss Parker, saying she would never have the letters typed in time for post. The man listened to the clicking of the machine for a few minutes and then set to work to finish his copy. But his head was not clear and his mind wandered away to the glare and rattle of the public-house. It was a night for hot punches. He struggled on with his copy, but when the clock struck five he had still fourteen pages to write. Blast it! He couldn't finish it in time. He longed to execrate aloud, to bring his fist down on something violently. He was so enraged that he wrote *Bernard Bernard* instead of *Bernard Bodley* and had to begin again on a clean sheet.

He felt strong enough to clear out the whole office single-handed. His body ached to do something, to rush out and revel in violence. All the indignities of his life enraged him. . . . Could he ask the cashier privately for an advance? No, the cashier was no good, no damn good: he wouldn't give an advance. . . . He knew where he would meet the boys: Leonard and O'Halloran and Nosey Flynn. The barometer of his emotional nature was set for a spell of riot.

His imagination had so abstracted him that his name was called twice before he answered. Mr. Alleyne and Miss Delacour were standing outside the counter and all the clerks had turned round in anticipation of something. The man got up from his desk. Mr. Alleyne began a tirade of abuse, saying that two letters were missing. The man answered that he knew nothing about them, that he had made a faithful copy. The tirade continued: it was so bitter and violent that the man could hardly restrain his fist from descending upon the head of the manikin before him:

"I know nothing about any other two letters," he said stupidly.

"*You–know–nothing*. Of course you know nothing," said Mr. Alleyne. "Tell me," he added, glancing first for approval to the lady beside him, "do you take me for a fool? Do you think me an utter fool?"

The man glanced from the lady's face to the little egg-shaped head and back again; and, almost before he was aware of it, his tongue had found a felicitous moment:

"I don't think, sir," he said, "that that's a fair question to put to me."

There was a pause in the very breathing of the clerks. Everyone was astounded (the author of the witticism no less than his neighbours) and Miss Delacour, who was a stout amiable person, began to smile broadly. Mr. Alleyne flushed to the hue of a wild rose and his mouth twitched with a dwarf's passion. He shook his fist in the man's face till it seemed to vibrate like the knob of some electric machine:

"You impertinent ruffian! You impertinent ruffian! I'll make short work of you! Wait till you see! You'll apologise to me for your impertinence or you'll quit the office instanter! You'll quit this, I'm telling you, or you'll apologise to me!"

He stood in a doorway opposite the office watching to see if the cashier would come out alone. All the clerks passed out and finally the cashier came out with the chief clerk. It was no use trying to say a word to him when he was with the chief clerk. The man felt that his position was bad enough. He had been obliged to offer an abject apology to Mr. Alleyne for his impertinence but he knew what a hornet's nest the office would be for him. He could remember the way in which Mr. Alleyne had hounded little Peake out of the office in order to make room for his own nephew. He felt savage and thirsty and revengeful, annoyed with himself and with everyone else. Mr. Alleyne would never give him an hour's rest; his life would be a hell to him. He had made a proper fool of himself this time. Could he not keep his tongue in his cheek? But they had never pulled together from the first, he and Mr. Alleyne, ever since the day Mr. Alleyne had overheard him mimicking his North of Ireland accent to amuse Higgins and Miss Parker: that had been the beginning of it. He might have tried Higgins for the money, but sure Higgins never had anything for himself. A man with two establishments to keep up, of course he couldn't. . . .

He felt his great body again aching for the comfort of the public-house. The fog had begun to chill him and he wondered could he touch Pat in O'Neill's. He could not touch him for more than a bob—and a bob was no use. Yet he must get money somewhere or other: he had spent his last penny for the g.p. and soon it would be too late for getting money anywhere. Suddenly, as he was fingering his watch-chain, he thought of Terry Kelly's pawn-office in Fleet Street. That was the dart! Why didn't he think of it sooner?

He went through the narrow alley of Temple Bar quickly, muttering to himself that they could all go to hell because he was going to have a good night of it. The clerk in Terry Kelly's said *A crown!* but the consignor held out for six shillings; and in the end the six shillings was allowed him literally. He came out of the pawn-office joyfully, making a little cylinder of the coins between his thumb and fingers. In Westmoreland Street the footpaths were crowded with young men and women returning from business and ragged urchins ran here and there yelling out the names of the evening editions. The man passed through the crowd, looking on the spectacle generally with proud satisfaction and staring masterfully at the office-girls. His head was full of the noises of tram-gongs and swishing trolleys and his nose already sniffed the curling fumes of punch. As he walked on he preconsidered the terms in which he would narrate the incident to the boys:

"So, I just looked at him—coolly, you know, and looked at her. Then I looked back at him again—taking my time, you know. 'I don't think that that's a fair question to put to me,' says I."

Nosey Flynn was sitting up in his usual corner of Davy Byrne's and, when he heard the story, he stood Farrington a half-one, saying it was as smart a thing as ever he heard. Farrington stood a drink in his turn. After a while O'Halloran and Paddy Leonard came in and the story was repeated to them. O'Halloran stood tailors of malt, hot, all round and told the story of the retort he had made to the chief clerk when he was in Callan's of Fownes's Street; but, as the retort was after the manner of the liberal shepherds in the eclogues, he had to admit that it was not as clever as Farrington's retort. At this Farrington told the boys to polish off that and have another.

Just as they were naming their poisons who should come in but Higgins! Of course he had to join in with the others. The men asked him to give his version of it, and he did so with great vivacity for the sight of five small hot whiskies was very exhilarating. Everyone roared laughing when he showed the way in which Mr. Alleyne shook his fist in Farrington's face. Then he imitated Farrington, saying, *"And here was my nabs, as cool as you please,"* while Farrington looked at the company out of his heavy dirty eyes, smiling and at times drawing forth stray drops of liquor from his moustache with the aid of his lower lip.

When that round was over there was a pause. O'Halloran had money but neither of the other two seemed to have any; so the whole party left the shop somewhat regretfully. At the corner of Duke Street Higgins and Nosey Flynn bevelled off to the left while the other three turned back towards the city. Rain was drizzling down on the cold streets and, when they reached the Ballast Office, Farrington suggested the Scotch House. The bar was full of men and loud with the noise of tongues and glasses. The three men pushed past the whining match-sellers at the door and formed a little party at the corner of the counter. They began to exchange stories. Leonard introduced them to a young fellow named Weathers who was performing at the Tivoli as an acrobat and knockabout *artiste.* Farrington stood a drink all round. Weathers said he would take a small Irish and Apollinaris. Farrington, who had definite notions of what was what, asked the boys would they have an Apollinaris too; but the boys told Tim to make theirs hot. The talk became theatrical. O'Halloran stood a round and then Farrington stood another round, Weathers protesting that the hospitality was too Irish. He promised to get them in behind the scenes and introduce them to some nice girls. O'Halloran said that he and Leonard would go, but that Farrington wouldn't go because he was a married man; and Farrington's heavy dirty eyes leered at the company in token that he understood he was being chaffed. Weathers made them all have just one little tincture at his expense and promised to meet them later on at Mulligan's in Poolbeg Street.

When the Scotch House closed they went round to Mulligan's. They went into the parlour at the back and O'Halloran ordered small hot specials all round. They were all beginning to feel mellow. Farrington was just standing another round when Weathers came back. Much to Farrington's relief he drank a glass of bitter this time. Funds were getting low but they had enough to keep them going. Presently two young women with big hats and a young man in a check suit came in and sat at a table close by. Weathers saluted them and told the company that they were out of the Tivoli. Farrington's eyes wandered at every moment in the direction of one of the young women. There was something striking in her appearance. An immense scarf of peacock-blue muslin was wound round her hat and knotted in a great bow under her chin; and she wore bright yellow gloves, reaching to the elbow. Farrington gazed admiringly at the plump arm which she moved very often and with much grace; and when, after a little time, she answered his gaze he admired still more her large dark brown eyes. The oblique staring expression in them fascinated him. She glanced at him once or twice and, when the party was leaving the room, she brushed against his chair and said *"O, pardon!"* in a London accent. He watched her leave the room in the hope that she would look back at him, but he was disappointed. He cursed his want of money and cursed all the rounds he had stood, particularly all the whiskies and Apollinaris which he had stood to Weathers. If there was one thing that he hated it was a sponge. He was so angry that he lost count of the conversation of his friends.

When Paddy Leonard called him he found that they were talking about feats of strength. Weathers was showing his biceps muscle to the company and boasting so much that the other two had called on Farrington to uphold the national honour. Farrington pulled up his sleeve accordingly and showed his biceps muscle to the company. The two arms were examined and compared and finally it was agreed to have a trial of strength. The table was cleared and the two men rested their elbows on it, clasping hands. When Paddy Leonard said *"Go!"* each was to try to bring down the other's hand on to the table. Farrington looked very serious and determined.

The trial began. After about thirty seconds Weathers brought his opponent's hand slowly down on to the table. Farrington's dark wine-coloured face flushed darker still with anger and humiliation at having been defeated by such a stripling.

"You're not to put the weight of your body behind it. Play fair," he said.

"Who's not playing fair?" said the other.

"Come on again. The two best out of three."

The trial began again. The veins stood out on Farrington's forehead, and the pallor of Weathers' complexion changed to peony. Their hands and arms trembled under the stress. After a long struggle Weathers again brought his opponent's hand slowly on to the table. There was a murmur of applause from the spectators. The curate, who was standing beside the table, nodded his red head towards the victor and said with stupid familiarity:

"Ah! that's the knack!"

"What the hell do you know about it?" said Farrington fiercely, turning on the man. "What do you put in your gab for?"

"Sh, sh!" said O'Halloran, observing the violent expression of Farrington's face. "Pony up, boys. We'll have just one little smahan more and then we'll be off."

A very sullen-faced man stood at the corner of O'Connell Bridge waiting for the little Sandymount tram to take him home. He was full of smouldering anger and revengefulness. He felt humiliated and discontented; he did not even feel drunk; and he had only twopence in his pocket. He cursed everything. He had done for himself in the office, pawned his watch, spent all his money; and he had not even got drunk. He began to feel thirsty again and he longed to be back again in the hot reeking public-house. He had lost his reputation as a strong man, having been defeated twice by a mere boy. His heart swelled with fury and, when he thought of the woman in the big hat who had brushed against him and said *Pardon!* his fury nearly choked him.

His tram let him down at Shelbourne Road and he steered his great body along in the shadow of the wall of the barracks. He loathed returning to his home. When he went in by the side-door he found the kitchen empty and the kitchen fire nearly out. He bawled upstairs:

"Ada! Ada!"

His wife was a little sharp-faced woman who bullied her husband when he was sober and was bullied by him when he was drunk. They had five children. A little boy came running down the stairs.

"Who is that?" said the man, peering through the darkness.

"Me, pa."

"Who are you? Charlie?"

"No, pa. Tom."

"Where's your mother?"

"She's out at the chapel."

"That's right. . . . Did she think of leaving any dinner for me?"

"Yes, pa. I—"

"Light the lamp. What do you mean by having the place in darkness? Are the other children in bed?"

The man sat down heavily on one of the chairs while the little boy lit the lamp. He began to mimic his son's flat accent, saying half to himself: *"At the chapel. At the chapel, if you please!"* When the lamp was lit he banged his fist on the table and shouted:

"What's for my dinner?"

"I'm going . . . to cook it, pa," said the little boy.

The man jumped up furiously and pointed to the fire.

"On that fire! You let the fire out! By God, I'll teach you to do that again!"

He took a step to the door and seized the walking-stick which was standing behind it.

"I'll teach you to let the fire out!" he said, rolling up his sleeve in order to give his arm free play.

The little boy cried "*O,pa*!" and ran whimpering round the table, but the man followed him and caught him by the coat. The little boy looked about him wildly but, seeing no way of escape, fell upon his knees.

"Now, you'll let the fire out the next time!" said the man, striking at him vigorously with the stick. "Take that, you little whelp!"

The boy uttered a squeal of pain as the stick cut his thigh. He clasped his hands together in the air and his voice shook with fright.

"O, pa!" he cried. "Don't beat me, pa! And I'll . . . I'll say a *Hail Mary* for you. . . . I'll say a *Hail Mary* for you, pa, if you don't beat me. . . . I'll say a *Hail Mary*. . . ."

The Chrysanthemums

John Steinbeck

The high grey-flannel fog of winter closed off the Salinas Valley from the sky and from all the rest of the world. On every side it sat like a lid on the mountains and made of the great valley a closed pot. On the broad, level land floor the gang plows bit deep and left the black earth shining like metal where the shares had cut. On the foothill ranches across the Salinas River, the yellow stubble fields seemed to be bathed in pale cold sunshine, but there was no sunshine in the valley now in December. The thick willow scrub along the river flamed with sharp and positive yellow leaves.

It was a time of quiet and of waiting. The air was cold and tender. A light wind blew up from the southwest so that the farmers were mildly hopeful of a good rain before long; but fog and rain do not go together.

Across the river, on Henry Allen's foothill ranch there was little work to be done, for the hay was cut and stored and the orchards were plowed up to receive the rain deeply when it should come. The cattle on the higher slopes were becoming shaggy and rough-coated.

Elisa Allen, working in her flower garden, looked down across the yard and saw Henry, her husband, talking to two men in business suits. The three of them stood by the tractor shed, each man with one foot on the side of the little Fordson. They smoked cigarettes and studied the machine as they talked.

Elisa watched them for a moment and then went back to her work. She was thirty-five. Her face was lean and strong and her eyes were as clear as water. Her figure looked blocked and heavy in her gardening costume, a man's black hat pulled low down over her eyes, clodhopper shoes, a figured print dress almost completely covered by a big corduroy apron with four big pockets to hold the snips, the trowel and scratcher, the seeds and the knife she worked with. She wore heavy leather gloves to protect her hands while she worked.

She was cutting down the old year's chrysanthemum stalks with a pair of short and powerful scissors. She looked down toward the men by the tractor shed now and then. Her face was eager and mature and handsome; even her work with the scissors was over-eager, over-powerful. The chrysanthemum stems seemed too small and easy for her energy.

She brushed a cloud of hair out of her eyes with the back of her glove, and left a smudge of earth on her cheek in doing it. Behind her stood the neat white farm house with red geraniums close-banked around it as high as the windows. It was a hard-swept looking little house with hard-polished windows, and a clean mud-mat on the front steps.

Elisa cast another glance toward the tractor shed. The strangers were getting into their Ford coupe. She took off a glove and put her strong fingers down into the forest of new green chrysanthemum sprouts that were growing around the old roots. She spread the leaves and looked down among the close-growing stems. No aphids were there, no sowbugs or snails or cutworms. Her terrier fingers destroyed such pests before they could get started.

Elisa started at the sound of her husband's voice. He had come near quietly, and he leaned over the wire fence that protected her flower garden from cattle and dogs and chickens.

"At it again," he said. "You've got a strong new crop coming."

Elisa straightened her back and pulled on the gardening glove again. "Yes. They'll be strong this coming year." In her tone and on her face there was a little smugness.

"You've got a gift with things," Henry observed. "Some of those yellow chrysanthemums you had this year were ten inches across. I wish you'd work out in the orchard and raise some apples that big."

Her eyes sharpened. "Maybe I could do it, too. I've a gift with things, all right. My mother had it. She could stick anything in the ground and make it grow. She said it was having planters' hands that knew how to do it."

"Well, it sure works with flowers," he said.

"Henry, who were those men you were talking to?"

"Why, sure, that's what I came to tell you. They were from the Western Meat Company. I sold those thirty head of three-year-old steers. Got nearly my own price, too."

"Good," she said. "Good for you."

"And I thought," he continued, "I thought how it's Saturday afternoon, and we might go into Salinas for dinner at a restaurant, and then to a picture show—to celebrate, you see."

"Good," she repeated. "Oh, yes. That will be good."

Henry put on his joking tone. "There's fights tonight. How'd you like to go to the fights?"

"Oh, no," she said breathlessly. "No, I wouldn't like fights."

"Just fooling, Elisa. We'll go to a movie. Let's see. It's two now. I'm going to take Scotty and bring down those steers from the hill. It'll take us maybe two hours. We'll go in town about five and have dinner at the Cominos Hotel. Like that?"

"Of course I'll like it. It's good to eat away from home."

"All right, then. I'll go get up a couple of horses."

She said, "I'll have plenty of time to transplant some of these sets, I guess."

She heard her husband calling Scotty down by the barn. And a little later she saw the two men ride up the pale yellow hillside in search of the steers.

There was a little square sandy bed kept for rooting the chrysanthemums. With her trowel she turned the soil over and over, and smoothed it and patted it firm. Then she dug ten parallel trenches to receive the sets. Back at the chrysanthemum bed she pulled out the little crisp shoots, trimmed off the leaves of each one with her scissors and laid it on a small orderly pile.

A squeak of wheels and plod of hoofs came from the road. Elisa looked up. The country road ran along the dense bank of willows and cottonwoods that bordered the river, and up this road came a curious vehicle, curiously drawn. It was an old spring-wagon, with a round canvas top on it like the cover of a prairie schooner. It was drawn by an old bay horse and a little grey-and-white burro. A big stubble-bearded man sat between the cover flaps and drove the crawling team. Underneath the wagon, between the hind wheels, a lean and rangy mongrel dog walked sedately. Words were painted on the canvas, in clumsy, crooked letters. "Pots, pans, knives, sisors, lawn mores, Fixed." Two rows of articles, and the triumphantly definitive "Fixed" below. The black paint had run down in little sharp points beneath each letter.

Elisa, squatting on the ground, watched to see the crazy, loose-jointed wagon pass by. But it didn't pass. It turned into the farm road in front of her house, crooked old wheels skirling and squeaking. The rangy dog darted from between the wheels and ran ahead. Instantly the two ranch shepherds flew out at him. Then all three stopped, and with stiff and quivering tails, with taut straight legs, with ambassadorial dignity, they slowly circled, sniffing daintily. The caravan pulled up to Elisa's wire fence and stopped. Now the newcomer dog, feeling out-numbered, lowered his tail and retired under the wagon with raised hackles and bared teeth.

The man on the wagon seat called out, "That's a bad dog in a fight when he gets started."

Elisa laughed. "I see he is. How soon does he generally get started?"

The man caught up her laughter and echoed it heartily. "Sometimes not for weeks and weeks," he said. He climbed stiffly down, over the wheel. The horse and the donkey drooped like unwatered flowers.

Elisa saw that he was a very big man. Although his hair and beard were greying, he did not look old. His worn black suit was wrinkled and spotted with grease. The laughter had disappeared from his face and eyes the moment his laughing voice ceased. His eyes were dark, and they were full of the brooding that gets in the eyes of teamsters and of sailors. The calloused hands he rested on the wire fence were cracked, and every crack was a black line. He took off his battered hat.

"I'm off my general road, ma'am," he said. "Does this dirt road cut over across the river to the Los Angeles highway?"

Elisa stood up and shoved the thick scissors in her apron pocket. "Well, yes, it does, but it winds around and then fords the river. I don't think your team could pull through the sand."

He replied with some asperity, "It might surprise you what them beasts can pull through."

"When they get started?" she asked.

He smiled for a second. "Yes. When they get started."

"Well," said Elisa, "I think you'll save time if you go back to the Salinas road and pick up the highway there."

He drew a big finger down the chicken wire and made it sing. "I ain't in any hurry, ma'am. I go from Seattle to San Diego and back every year. Takes all my time. About six months each way. I aim to follow nice weather."

Elisa took off her gloves and stuffed them in the apron pocket with the scissors. She touched the under edge of her man's hat, searching for fugitive hairs. "That sounds like a nice kind of a way to live," she said.

He leaned confidentially over the fence. "Maybe you noticed the writing on my wagon. I mend pots and sharpen knives and scissors. You got any of them things to do?"

"Oh, no," she said quickly. "Nothing like that." Her eyes hardened with resistance.

"Scissors is the worst thing," he explained. "Most people just ruin scissors trying to sharpen 'em, but I know how. I got a special tool. It's a little bobbit kind of thing, and patented. But it sure does the trick."

"No. My scissors are all sharp."

"All right, then. Take a pot," he continued earnestly, "a bent pot, or a pot with a hole. I can make it like new so you don't have to buy no new ones. That's a saving for you."

"No," she said shortly. "I tell you I have nothing like that for you to do."

His face fell to an exaggerated sadness. His voice took on a whining undertone. "I ain't had a thing to do today. Maybe I won't have no supper tonight. You see I'm off my regular road. I know folks on the highway clear from Seattle to San Diego. They save their things for me to sharpen up because they know I do it so good and save them money."

"I'm sorry," Elisa said irritably. "I haven't anything for you to do."

His eyes left her face and fell to searching the ground. They roamed about until they came to the chrysanthemum bed where she had been working. "What's them plants, ma'am?"

The irritation and resistance melted from Elisa's face. "Oh, those are chrysanthemums, giant whites and yellows. I raise them every year, bigger than anybody around here."

"Kind of a long-stemmed flower? Looks like a quick puff of colored smoke?" he asked.

"That's it. What a nice way to describe them."

"They smell kind of nasty till you get used to them," he said.

"It's a good bitter smell," she retorted, "not nasty at all."

He changed his tone quickly. "I like the smell myself."

"I had ten-inch blooms this year," she said.

The man leaned farther over the fence. "Look. I know a lady down the road a piece, has got the nicest garden you ever seen. Got nearly every kind of flower but no chrysanthemums. Last time I was mending a copper-bottom washtub for her (that's a hard job but I do it good), she said to me, 'If you ever run acrost some nice chrysanthemums I wish you'd try to get me a few seeds.' That's what she told me."

Elisa's eyes grew alert and eager. "She couldn't have known much about chrysanthemums. You *can* raise them from seed, but it's much easier to root the little sprouts you see there."

"Oh," he said. "I s'pose I can't take none to her, then."

"Why yes you can," Elisa cried. "I can put some in damp sand, and you can carry them right along with you. They'll take root in the pot if you keep them damp. And then she can transplant them."

"She'd sure like to have some, ma'am. You say they're nice ones?"

"Beautiful," she said. "Oh, beautiful." Her eyes shone. She tore off the battered hat and shook out her dark pretty hair. "I'll put them in a flower pot, and you can take them right with you. Come into the yard."

While the man came through the picket gate Elisa ran excitedly along the geranium-bordered path to the back of the house. And she returned carrying a big red flower pot. The gloves were forgotten now. She kneeled on the ground by the starting bed and dug up the sandy soil with her fingers and scooped it into the bright new flower pot. Then she picked up the little pile of shoots she had prepared. With her strong fingers she pressed them into the sand and tamped around them with her knuckles. The man stood over her. "I'll tell you what to do," she said. "You remember so you can tell the lady."

"Yes, I'll try to remember."

"Well, look. These will take root in about a month. Then she must set them out, about a foot apart in good rich earth like this, see?" She lifted a handful of dark soil for him to look at. "They'll grow fast and tall. Now remember this: In July tell her to cut them down, about eight inches from the ground."

"Before they bloom?" he asked.

"Yes, before they bloom." Her face was tight with eagerness. "They'll grow right up again. About the last of September the buds will start."

She stopped and seemed perplexed. "It's the budding that takes the most care," she said hesitantly. "I don't know how to tell you." She looked deep into his eyes, searchingly. Her mouth opened a little, and she seemed to be listening. "I'll try to tell you," she said. "Did you ever hear of planting hands?"

"Can't say I have, ma'am."

"Well, I can only tell you what it feels like. It's when you're picking off the buds you don't want. Everything goes right down into your fingertips. You watch your fingers work. They do it themselves. You can feel how it is. They pick and pick the buds. They never make a mistake. They're with the plant. Do you see? Your fingers and the plant. You can feel that, right up your arm. They know. They never make a mistake. You can feel it. When you're like that you can't do anything wrong. Do you see that? Can you understand that?"

She was kneeling on the ground looking up at him. Her breast swelled passionately.

The man's eyes narrowed. He looked away self-consciously. "Maybe I know," he said. "Sometimes in the night in the wagon there—"

Elisa's voice grew husky. She broke in on him, "I've never lived as you do, but I know what you mean. When the night is dark—why, the stars are sharp-pointed, and there's quiet. Why, you rise up and up! Every pointed star gets driven into your body. It's like that. Hot and sharp and—lovely."

Kneeling there, her hand went out toward his legs in the greasy black trousers. Her hesitant fingers almost touched the cloth. Then her hand dropped to the ground. She crouched low like a fawning dog.

He said, "It's nice, just like you say. Only when you don't have no dinner, it ain't."

She stood up then, very straight, and her face was ashamed. She held the flower pot out to him and placed it gently in his arms. "Here. Put it in your wagon, on the seat, where you can watch it. Maybe I can find something for you to do."

At the back of the house she dug in the can pile and found two old and battered aluminum saucepans. She carried them back and gave them to him. "Here, maybe you can fix these."

His manner changed. He became professional. "Good as new I can fix them." At the back of his wagon he set a little anvil, and out of an oily tool box dug a small machine hammer. Elisa came through the gate to watch him while he pounded out the dents in the kettles. His mouth grew sure and knowing. At a difficult part of the work he sucked his under-lip.

"You sleep right in the wagon?" Elisa asked.

"Right in the wagon, ma'am. Rain or shine I'm dry as a cow in there."

"It must be nice," she said. "It must be very nice. I wish women could do such things."

"It ain't the right kind of a life for a woman."

Her upper lip raised a little, showing her teeth. "How do you know? How can you tell?" she said.

"I don't know, ma'am," he protested. "Of course I don't know. Now here's your kettles, done. You don't have to buy no new ones."

"How much?"

"Oh, fifty cents'll do. I keep my prices down and my work good. That's why I have all them satisfied customers up and down the highway."

Elisa brought him a fifty-cent piece from the house and dropped it in his hand. "You might be surprised to have a rival some time. I can sharpen scissors, too. And I can beat the dents out of little pots. I could show you what a woman might do."

He put his hammer back in the oily box and shoved the little anvil out of sight. "It would be a lonely life for a woman, ma'am, and a scarey life, too, with animals creeping under the wagon all night." He climbed over the singletree, steadying himself with a hand on the burro's white rump. He settled himself in the seat, picked up the lines. "Thank you kindly, ma'am," he said. "I'll do like you told me; I'll go back and catch the Salinas road."

"Mind," she called, "if you're long in getting there, keep the sand damp."

"Sand, ma'am? . . . Sand? Oh, sure. You mean around the chrysanthemums. Sure I will." He clucked his tongue. The beasts leaned luxuriously into their collars. The mongrel dog took his place between the back wheels. The wagon turned and crawled out the entrance road and back the way it had come, along the river.

Elisa stood in front of her wire fence watching the slow progress of the caravan. Her shoulders were straight, her head thrown back, her eyes half-closed, so that the scene came vaguely into them. Her lips moved silently, forming the words "Good-bye–good-bye." Then she whispered, "That's a bright direction. There's a glowing there."

The sound of her whisper startled her. She shook herself free and looked about to see whether anyone had been listening. Only the dogs had heard. They lifted their heads toward her from their sleeping in the dust, and then stretched out their chins and settled asleep again. Elisa turned and ran hurriedly into the house.

In the kitchen she reached behind the stove and felt the water tank. It was full of hot water from the noonday cooking. In the bathroom she tore off her soiled clothes and flung them into the corner. And then she scrubbed herself with a little block of pumice, legs and thighs, loins and chest and arms, until her skin was scratched and red. When she had dried herself she stood in front of a mirror in her bedroom and looked at her body. She tightened her stomach and threw out her chest. She turned and looked over her shoulder at her back.

After a while she began to dress, slowly. She put on her newest underclothing and her nicest stockings and the dress which was the symbol of her prettiness. She worked carefully on her hair, penciled her eyebrows and rouged her lips.

Before she was finished she heard the little thunder of hoofs and the shouts of Henry and his helper as they drove the red steers into the corral. She heard the gate bang shut and set herself for Henry's arrival.

His step sounded on the porch. He entered the house calling, "Elisa, where are you?"

"In my room, dressing. I'm not ready. There's hot water for your bath. Hurry up. It's getting late."

When she heard him splashing in the tub, Elisa laid his dark suit on the bed, and shirt and socks and tie beside it. She stood his polished shoes on the floor beside the bed. Then she went to the porch and sat primly and stiffly down. She looked toward the river road where the willow-line was still yellow with frosted leaves so that under the high grey fog they seemed a thin band of sunshine. This was the only color in the grey afternoon. She sat unmoving for a long time. Her eyes blinked rarely.

Henry came banging out of the door, shoving his tie inside his vest as he came. Elisa stiffened and her face grew tight. Henry stopped short and looked at her. "Why–why, Elisa. You look so nice!"

"Nice? You think I look nice? What do you mean by 'nice'?"

Henry blundered on. "I don't know. I mean you look different, strong and happy."

"I am strong? Yes, strong. What do you mean 'strong'?"

He looked bewildered. "You're playing some kind of a game," he said helplessly. "It's a kind of a play. You look strong enough to break a calf over your knee, happy enough to eat it like a watermelon."

For a second she lost her rigidity. "Henry! Don't talk like that. You didn't know what you said." She grew complete again. "I'm strong," she boasted. "I never knew before how strong."

Henry looked down toward the tractor shed, and when he brought his eyes back to her, they were his own again. "I'll get out the car. You can put on your coat while I'm starting."

Elisa went into the house. She heard him drive to the gate and idle down his motor, and then she took a long time to put on her hat. She pulled it here and pressed it there. When Henry turned the motor off she slipped into her coat and went out.

The little roadster bounced along on the dirt road by the river, raising the birds and driving the rabbits into the brush. Two cranes flapped heavily over the willow-line and dropped into the river-bed.

Far ahead on the road Elisa saw a dark speck. She knew.

She tried not to look as they passed it, but her eyes would not obey. She whispered to herself sadly, "He might have thrown them off the road. That wouldn't have been much trouble, not very much. But he kept the pot," she explained. "He had to keep the pot. That's why he couldn't get them off the road."

The roadster turned a bend and she saw the caravan ahead. She swung full around toward her husband so she could not see the little covered wagon and the mismatched team as the car passed them.

In a moment it was over. The thing was done. She did not look back.

She said loudly, to be heard above the motor, "It will be good, tonight, a good dinner."

"Now you're changed again," Henry complained. He took one hand from the wheel and patted her knee. "I ought to take you in to dinner oftener. It would be good for both of us. We get so heavy out on the ranch."

"Henry," she asked, "could we have wine at dinner?"

"Sure we could. Say! That will be fine."

She was silent for a while; then she said, "Henry, at those prize fights, do the men hurt each other very much?"

"Sometimes a little, not often. Why?"

"Well, I've read how they break noses, and blood runs down their chests. I've read how the fighting gloves get heavy and soggy with blood."

He looked around at her. "What's the matter, Elisa? I didn't know you read things like that." He brought the car to a stop, then turned to the right over the Salinas River bridge.

"Do any women ever go to the fights?" she asked.

"Oh, sure, some. What's the matter, Elisa? Do you want to go? I don't think you'd like it, but I'll take you if you really want to go."

She relaxed limply in the seat. "Oh, no. No. I don't want to go. I'm sure I don't." Her face was turned away from him. "It will be enough if we can have wine. It will be plenty." She turned up her coat collar so he could not see that she was crying weakly—like an old woman.

Son in the Afternoon

John A. Williams

It was hot. I tend to be a bitch when it's hot. I goosed the little Ford over Sepulveda Boulevard toward Santa Monica until I got stuck in the traffic that pours from L. A. into the surrounding towns. I'd had a very lousy day at the studio.

I was—still am—a writer and this studio had hired me to check scripts and films with Negroes in them to make sure the Negro movie-goer wouldn't be offended. The signs were already clear one day the whole of American industry would be racing pellmell to get a Negro, showcase a spade. I was kind of a pioneer. I'm a *Negro* writer, you see. The day had been tough because of a couple of verbs—slink and walk. One of those Hollywood hippies had done a script calling for a Negro waiter to slink away from the table where a dinner party was glaring at him. I said the waiter should walk, not slink, because later on he becomes a hero. The Hollywood hippie, who understood it all because he had some colored friends, said that it was essential to the plot that the waiter slink. I said you don't slink one minute and become a hero the next; there has to be some consistency. The Negro actor I was standing up for said nothing either way. He had played Uncle Tom roles so long that he had become Uncle Tom. But the director agreed with me.

Anyway . . . hear me out now. I was on my way to Santa Monica to pick up my mother, Nora. It was a long haul for such a hot day. I had planned a quiet evening: a nice shower, fresh clothes, and then I would have dinner at the Watkins and talk with some of the musicians on the scene for a quick taste before they cut to their gigs.

After, I was going to the Pigalle down on Figueroa and catch Earl Grant at the organ, and still later, if nothing exciting happened, I'd pick up Scottie and make it to the Lighthouse on the Beach or to the Strollers and listen to some of the white boys play. I liked the long drive, especially while listening to Sleepy Stein's show on the radio. Later, much later of course, it would be home, back to Watts.

So you see, this picking up Nora was a little inconvenient. My mother was a maid for the Couchmans. Ronald Couchman was an architect, a good one I understood from Nora who has a fine sense for this sort of thing; you don't work in some hundred-odd houses during your life without getting some idea of the way a house should be laid out. Couchman's wife, Kay, was a playgirl who drove a white Jaguar from one party to another. My mother didn't like her too much; she didn't seem to care much for her son, Ronald, junior. There's something wrong with a parent who can't really love her own child, Nora thought. The Couchmans lived in a real fine residential section, of course. A number of actors lived nearby, character actors, not really big stars.

Somehow it is very funny. I mean that the maids and butlers knew everything about these people, and these people knew nothing at all about the help. Through Nora and her friends I knew who was laying whose wife; who had money and who *really* had money; I knew about the wild parties hours before the police, and who smoked marijuana, when, and where they got it.

To get to Couchman's driveway I had to go three blocks up one side of a palm-planted center strip and back down the other. The driveway bent gently, then swept back out of sight of the main road. The house, sheltered by slim palms, looked like a transplanted New England Colonial. I parked and walked to the kitchen door, skirting the growling Great Dane who was tied to a tree. That was the route to the kitchen door.

I don't like kitchen doors. Entering people's houses by them, I mean. I'd done this thing most of my life when I called at places where Nora worked to pick up the patched or worn sheets or the half-eaten roasts, the battered, tarnished silver—the fringe benefits of a housemaid. As a teen-ager I'd told Nora I was through with that crap; I was not going through anyone's kitchen door. She only laughed and said I'd learn. One day soon after, I called for her and without knocking walked right through the front door of this house and right on through the living room. I was almost out of the room when I saw feet behind the couch. I leaned over and there was Mr. Jorgensen and his wife making out like crazy. I guess they thought Nora had gone and it must have hit them sort of suddenly and they went at it like the hell-bomb was due to drop any minute. I've been that way too, mostly in the spring. Of course, when Mr. Jorgensen looked over his shoulder and saw me, you know what happened. I was thrown out and Nora right behind me. It was the middle of winter, the old man was sick and the coal bill three months overdue. Nora was right about those kitchen doors: I learned.

My mother saw me before I could ring the bell. She opened the door. "Hello," she said. She was breathing hard, like she'd been running or something. "Come in and sit down. I don't know *where* that Kay is. Little Ronald is sick and she's probably out gettin' drunk again." She left me then and trotted back through the house, I guess to be with Ronnie. I hated the combination of her white nylon uniform, her dark brown face and the wide streaks of gray in her hair. Nora had married this guy from Texas a few years after the old man had died. He was all right. He made out okay. Nora didn't have to work, but she just couldn't be still; she always had to be doing something. I suggested she quit work, but I had as much luck as her husband. I used to tease her about liking to be around those white folks. It would have been good for her to take an extended trip around the country visiting my brothers and sisters. Once she got to Philadelphia, she could go right out to the cemetery and sit awhile with the old man.

I walked through the Couchman home. I liked the library. I thought if I knew Couchman I'd like him. The room made me feel like that. I left it and went into the big living room. You could tell that Couchman had let his wife do that. Everything in it was fast, dart-like, with no sense of ease. But on the walls were several of Couchman's conceptions of buildings and homes. I guess he was a disciple of Wright. My mother walked rapidly through the room without looking at me and said, "Just be patient, Wendell. She should be here real soon."

"Yeah," I said, "with a snootful." I had turned back to the drawings when Ronnie scampered into the room, his face twisted with rage.

"Nora!" he tried to roar, perhaps the way he'd seen the parents of some of his friends roar at their maids. I'm quite sure Kay didn't shout at Nora, and I don't think Couchman would. But then no one shouts at Nora. "Nora, you come right back here this minute!" the little bastard shouted and stamped and pointed to a spot on the floor where Nora was supposed to come to roost. I have a nasty temper. Sometimes it lies dormant for ages and at other times, like when the weather is hot and nothing seems to be going right, it's bubbling and ready to explode. "Don't talk to *my* mother like that, you little–!" I said sharply, breaking off just before I cursed. I wanted him to be large enough for me to strike. "How'd you like for me to talk to *your* mother like that?"

The nine-year-old looked up at me in surprise and confusion. He hadn't expected me to say anything. I was just another piece of furniture. Tears rose in his eyes and spilled out onto his pale cheeks. He put his hands behind him, twisted them. He moved backwards, away from me. He looked at my mother with a "Nora, come help me" look. And sure enough, there was Nora, speeding back across the room, gathering the kid in her arms, tucking his robe together. I was too angry to feel hatred for myself.

Ronnie was the Couchman's only kid. Nora loved him. I suppose that was the trouble. Couchman was gone ten, twelve hours a day. Kay didn't stay around the house any longer than she had to. So Ronnie had only my mother. I think kids should have someone to love, and Nora wasn't a bad sort. But somehow when the six of us, her own children, were growing up we never had her. She was gone, out scuffling to get those crumbs to put into our mouths and shoes for our feet and praying for something to happen so that all the space in between would be taken care of. Nora's affection for us took the form of rushing out into the morning's five o'clock blackness to wake some silly bitch and get her coffee; took form in her trudging five miles home every night instead of taking the streetcar to save money to buy tablets for us, to use at school, we said. But the truth was that all of us liked to draw and we went through a writing tablet in a couple of hours every day. Can you imagine? There's not a goddamn artist among us. We never had the physical affection, the pat on the head, the quick, smiling kiss, the "gimmee a hug" routine. All of this Ronnie was getting.

Now he buried his little blond head in Nora's breast and sobbed. "There, there now," Nora said. "Don't you cry, Ronnie. Ol' Wendell is just jealous, and he hasn't much sense either. He didn't mean nuthin'."

I left the room. Nora had hit it of course, hit it and passed on. I looked back. It didn't look so incongruous, the white and black together, I mean. Ronnie was still sobbing. His head bobbed gently on Nora's shoulder. The only time I ever got that close to her was when she trapped me with a bearhug so she could whale the daylights out of me after I put a snowball through Mrs. Grant's window. I walked outside and lit a cigarette. When Ronnie was in the hospital the month before, Nora got me to run her way over to Hollywood every night to see him. I didn't like that worth a damn. All right, I'll admit it: it did upset me. All that affection I didn't get nor my brothers and sisters going to that little white boy who, without a doubt, when away from her called her the names he'd learned from adults. Can you imagine a nine-year-old kid calling Nora a "girl," "our girl?" I spat at the Great Dane. He snarled and then I bounced a rock off his fanny. "Lay down, you bastard," I muttered. It was a good thing he was tied up.

I heard the low cough of the Jaguar slapping against the road. The car was throttled down, and with a muted roar it swung into the driveway. The woman aimed it for me. I was evil enough not to move. I was tired of playing with these people. At the last moment, grinning, she swung the wheel over and braked. She bounded out of the car like a tennis player vaulting over a net.

"Hi," she said, tugging at her shorts.

"Hello."

"You're Nora's boy?"

"I'm Nora's son." Hell, I was as old as she was; besides, I can't stand "boy."

"Nora tells us you're working in Hollywood. Like it?"

"It's all right."

"You must be pretty talented."

We stood looking at each other while the dog whined for her attention. Kay had a nice body and it was well tanned. She was high, boy, was she high. Looking at her, I could feel myself going into my sexy bastard routine; sometimes I can swing it great. Maybe it all had to do with the business inside. Kay took off her sunglasses and took a good look at me. "Do you have a cigarette?"

I gave her one and lit it. "Nice tan," I said. Most white people I know think it's a great big deal if a Negro compliments them on their tans. It's a large laugh. You have all this volleyball about color and come summer you can't hold the white folks back from the beaches, anyplace where they can get some sun. And of course the blacker they get, the more pleased they are. Crazy. If there is ever a Negro revolt, it will come during the summer and Negroes will descend upon the beaches around the nation and paralyze the country. You can't conceal cattle prods and bombs and pistols and police dogs when you're showing your birthday suit to the sun.

"You like it?" she asked. She was pleased. She placed her arm next to mine. "Almost the same color," she said.

"Ronnie isn't feeling well," I said.

"Oh, the poor kid. I'm so glad we have Nora. She's such a charm. I'll run right in and look at him. Do have a drink in the bar. Fix me one too, will you?" Kay slipped inside and I went to the bar and poured out two strong drinks. I made hers stronger than mine. She was back soon. "Nora was trying to put him to sleep and she made me stay out." She giggled. She quickly tossed off her drink. "Another, please?" While I was fixing her drink she was saying how amazing it was for Nora to have such a talented son. What she was really saying was that it was amazing for a servant to have a son who was not also a servant. "Anything can happen in a democracy," I said. "Servants' sons drink with madames and so on."

"Oh, Nora isn't a servant," Kay said. "She's part of the family."

Yeah, I thought. Where and how many times had I heard *that* before?

In the ensuing silence, she started to admire her tan again. "You think it's pretty good, do you? You don't know how hard I worked to get it." I moved close to her and held her arm. I placed my other arm around her. She pretended not to see or feel it, but she wasn't trying to get away either. In fact she was pressing closer and the register in my brain that tells me at the precise moment when I'm in, went off. Kay was very high. I put both arms around her and she put both hers around me. When I kissed her, she responded completely.

"Mom!"

"Ronnie, come back to bed," I heard Nora shout from the other room. We could hear Ronnie running over the rug in the outer room. Kay tried to get away from me, push me to one side, because we could tell that Ronnie knew where to look for his Mom: he was running right for the bar, where we were. "Oh, please," she said, "don't let him see us." I wouldn't let her push me away. "Stop!" she hissed. "He'll *see* us!" We stopped struggling just for an instant, and we listened to the echoes of the word *see*. She gritted her teeth and renewed her efforts to get away.

Me? I had the scene laid right out. The kid breaks into the room, see, and sees his mother in this real wriggly clinch with this colored guy who's just shouted at him, see, and no matter how his mother explains it away, the kid has the image—the colored guy and his mother—for the rest of his life, see?

That's the way it happened. The kid's mother hissed under her breath. *"You're crazy!"* and she looked at me as though she were seeing me or something about me for the very first time. I'd released her as soon as Ronnie, romping into the bar, saw us and came to a full, open-mouthed halt. Kay turned to me, but she couldn't speak.

Outside in the living room my mother called, "Wendell, where are you? We can go now."

I started to move past Kay and Ronnie. I felt many things, but I made myself think mostly, *There you little bastard, there.*

My mother thrust her face inside the door and said, "Good-bye, Mrs. Couchman. See you tomorrow. 'Bye, Ronnie."

"Yes," Kay said, sort of stunned. "Tomorrow." She was reaching for Ronnie's hand as we left, but the kid was slapping her hand away. I hurried quickly after Nora, hating the long drive back to Watts.

Coming Home

George Davis

STACY

I come into the red wooden shower house. It is up on piles to keep snakes—cobras, vipers—from crawling up the drains.

Childress is there already with the water coming down over his head. Above the roar of the water, he says: "I'm not going to let a Harvard-trained nigger inherit the best whore in Thailand."

I repeat it: "So you're not . . ." I say. I do not want to say nigger because I don't know if he'd like hearing a white person say it. I drop my shower clogs out the door into the sand.

"Nope," he says. The water is coming down over him, beating the top of his head, pulling the curls out of his slightly Negroid hair. He opens his mouth and lets water flow into it.

"Why?"

"I don't know," he says as he stops soaping himself and stares for a moment. "I don't know."

I watch him and say to myself: why, if you're back in America and don't give a damn about Thailand or Asia or the Vietnam War?

He gets out of the shower and starts to dry himself on a large green towel. I come out and down the stairs too. His brown skin is a little grayish from all the water that has run over it. He must have been in the shower a long time before I woke up. Grayish like his mouth is sometimes when he comes down from flying and takes his oxygen mask off. Gray and greaseless.

"She's been with me six months," he says. "For some reason it just wouldn't feel right, him having her."

"So you got a way to stop him?" I ask.

"No. But I'll think of something before I go."

"You'd better hurry and dry off. We only got fifteen minutes."

"What time is briefing?"

"Thirteen past. You wouldn't want to be late for your last run."

"Yea. I got to go kill my last Gook."

I stare at him as he continues to dry himself. He is heavy but muscular. His toes are curled up to keep them out of the sand.

"Either you or Ben in my flight?" he asks.

"No, Ben's earlier and I'm about a half-hour later."

"Too bad, I'd like for one of you to see-me-do-it this one, last time."

I start across the sand, walking along a path which separates the beach from the reedy jungle. The towel hangs around my waist. Dozens of pilots come out of their tents and out of the other small raised shower-houses. Childress follows me along the path.

BEN

A dump truck wakes me. Noisily the truck plows along the dusty road beside the tent, groaning. Another truck follows. I open one eye and watch them through the screen at the side of the tent. The wheels pick up dust and throw it off like water off the prow of a boat. Soon they will finish the new runways they are building down near the gulf, I think.

Stacy's and Childress' cots are empty. I think about Childress singing in the shower. I think about this being his last mission, and about me getting to know his girl, Damg, after he goes back to the States. For a moment I wonder how it would work out if I took her back with me. Marry her. I would marry her. I push myself deep into the mattress on my cot. Twenty more missions for me. Eighty gone. I wonder how many people I have killed. I never think about killing unless I consciously decide to think about killing. Childress must never think about it. I must be more lost than he is, more self-divided, or maybe he is more self-divided than me, less aware of his other human self. Rhyme. No.

I pull myself out of the bed and smother my face in my hands, trying to seal my nose from some of the dust that the sun seems to beat out of the canvas tent top. Already the day is hot. I don't feel like taking a shower. I have sweated in my bed and I feel funky in my pits and groin. I feel the sweat, perspiration, a Harvard man would say, along the side of my body and along the inside of both arms so that my arms stick to my body when I press them against me. I feel myself funky. I feel funky. As if funky. Through the door I see a bulldozer pushing down a section of the jungle where they are going to build the oil storage tanks. Past that I see treetops wavering and then falling and I think of the barefooted Thais at the bases of the trees chopping away, clearing a site for the permanent quarters near the barbwire fence. To me the barbwire is as much to lock us in as it is to keep the Asians out.

I take a still-damp towel and wipe my face. I wonder what it will be like having a whore who can speak English. I wonder what it will be like getting to know Asia through her. In a way I will be glad to see Childress leave. I would marry her, yes.

My boots are scuffed. I look down at them and try to think about napalm because I want to think about dropping napalm. The floor of the tent is rough. I jam my feet into the hollowed-out innersole of my boots. Time for briefing. I stand and visualize myself standing naked in my boots. Then I slip dirty undershorts over my boots and pull them up. Then I slip on my flight fatigues. No one can see that I am flying with no socks on. If I get shot down over the mountains, my feet will freeze. I never think about getting shot down.

I leave the tent.

CHILDRESS

The war is changing Stacy, or was he that way when he came into the war. I sit on the side of my cot and dry my feet. Maybe he always was a silly-ass white boy. Otherwise why would he want to room with the only two niggerflyers in the outfit. Hippie-type motherfucker. One of these times I'm going to catch him in the tent singing folk songs.

Ben's gone. Stacy's gone. I look at my watch and laugh. My last motherfucker. Boots untied, I run across to the briefing room.

STACY

The bench is hard against my haunches. The Air Force has enough money to put backs on the benches. They don't want people to get comfortable enough to sleep, I think. I am not sleepy.

Captain Peterson is briefing. He briefs the primary targets. Weather is always bad over primary. We always go first alternate because the weather over primary will not be good until April. Peterson leans forward. His face is bathed in the fluorescent light from the podium lamp. I hate the briefing because I have heard it sixty to seventy times. Peterson has given it two hundred times, but he seems not to notice.

"One-quarter mile visibility with thunder bumpers over primary," Peterson says.

I squirm on my bench. Childress stiffens against me after I rock into him. "We ain't going primary," he whispers out of the side of his mouth.

"I know," I say.

"Tell Peterson, the ass."

"Let the bastard do his duty," I say. I think Peterson lives by rote. I watch his dumb lower jaw move. He has a round, reddish face that looks redder yet in the fluorescent light. The red EXIT bulb is the only other light in the room.

I am better-looking than Peterson. He has blond hair. Most girls would think that he is better-looking because he has blond hair. He looks like he dyes his hair.

He turns on the squawk-box and the weatherman's voice booms into the darkened room. "Weather over primary: one hundred foot overcast, one-quarter mile visibility with towering cumulus . . ." Peterson snaps on a little light above a weather chart. He moves his pointer robot-like across an area just north of Hanoi.

The weatherman's voice is so loud it is distorted. "Any questions?"

No one asks. Peterson comes back into the podium light. The weatherman gives the weather over alternate. Peterson does not point to this area. Pleiku, but I watch it. "Any questions?"

No one speaks. Peterson's head moves out of the light as he puts his pointer down. His wife probably makes him dye his hair. His stupid, little, tight-titted, faithful wife who probably wants blond children.

Childress rocks against me. "No anti-aircraft guns," he whispers.

"Is that what he said?"

"Sure, you know they don't have any in the Pleiku area." Childress laughs.

There is something that I've never really liked about Childress, and it's not a color thing either because I like Ben; but deep down I don't think Ben likes white people.

Peterson's jaw looks dead and heavy as if he has just gotten out of the dentist's chair. "You are executed alternate mission," he says.

My spine is tired from sitting on the backless bench. I stiffen and concave my spine, hoping to put some of my weight on my stomach muscles. I know my back will get sorer yet when I put my parachute on. If I never see an F-105 after this war I'll be happy.

"Any questions?" Peterson asks. We are already out of our seats, milling toward the door.

CHILDRESS

I say: "Red Dog 2 is ready for takeoff." I watch to see when Red Dog 1 releases brakes. His nose gear tire is a little flat on the runway. I begin to sweat almost as if I had not taken a shower. Heat from the sun and the jet engines of the planes–F-105's and tankers–that have taken off before us bounces up from the slab of concrete. Number 1 fires his afterburners sending flames out in back of him. Smoke drifts across my windshield.

I feel almost guilty having an easy one for my last. But there is always a chance that some lucky son-of-a-bitch will get me with ground-fire.

Red Dog 1 releases brakes. I release. We roll.

I break ground and climb fast to catch Red Dog 1 as he levels his wings to climb straight out. I can see Red Dog 3 closing on me from the left. Red Dog 4 is sliding into position beside him. Sunshine flashes off number 1's wings and he looks like a silver bullet in the empty blue sky.

My radio is garbled. If there is a MIG warning I wouldn't hear it, but there are no MIG's down where we are going. Only some lucky son-of-a-bitch on the ground has a chance of getting me. I nudge my throttles.

"Red Dog 1 changing frequencies," number 1 says.

"Red Dog 2, changing," I say.

"3, changing," number 3 says.

"4."

After we change frequencies I can hear better. We start eastward along the Cambodian border. There is a light haze across the landscape.

For a moment I almost wish that I would see a MIG so I could get me one before I go home. Win another medal. Take it back to Baltimore and wave it in the man's face.

When he says: "Boy . . ." I'll say: "Boy, my ass," and slap him across the nose with one of my medals.

"Turning," Red Dog 1 says.

"Turning," I say and tuck in close in the turn. I look down through the haze and try to locate the large lake north of Phnom Penh, but it is too far away and a little behind us. I strain to look back over my shoulder then I turn around to keep number 1 in sight. The Mekong River is barely visible ahead of us, and I watch it as it seems to slide in our direction until it is directly below us, and I think that after today I will never see the river again. We fly south where the river spreads out like a giant swamp. I rock my wings and look down.

"Turning," number 1 says.

"Turning."

"Turning."

"Turning."

The forward air controller is southeast of us and we take up a course to the southeast toward him. His radio is good.

I see him below us, flying slow just above the treetops. The trees lie like a hedge field beneath him, and he seems to hang blue-silver and motionless above the hedges.

"Do you have enough fuel to work with me a half-hour?" he asks.

Red Dog 1 says: "We can stay for a half-hour."

"That should be enough. Do you have four birds?"

"Roger, four chicks," Red Dog 1 says.

Forward air controller directs us south toward our target. Mare's-tail clouds lay between us and a flat narrow road which zigzags out of the mountains off to our right and runs straight toward the river before it disappears into a swamp.

We make a low pass to take a look, then pull up to wait for forward air controller to drop a smoke marker where he wants us to hit. We come back across flying northeast and see bright orange smoke from the marker drifting up out of the forest.

Forward air controller says some Gooks in trucks pulled off the road northeast of the smoke. We come back across flying southeast. The lush foliage is thick enough to hide something as large as a group of trucks. I try to spy the path that they made getting off the road, but the jungle has enveloped everything. We streak across too fast for me to see much, but I wonder if there is some lucky son-of-a-bitch down there in the trees waiting for me.

Red Dog 1 and I come in first. Number 1 lays his bomb close to the road. I come across. My stomach is knotted, tensed for the first burst of machine-gun fire. I put mine closer to the smoke and pull up too soon to see if we have knocked anything loose. Three more to go. No machine-gun fire, yet.

Number 1 and I climb and circle back while 3 and 4 come across. I think that the Gooks must be trying to make us think that they are not down there.

I watch my instruments as I come down again, lower, and I wait for some unseen hole in the treetops to begin cracking with machine-gun fire. Red Dog 1 has hit on the road. I oblique to him, pull level and let the hedge-green trees shoot under me. Then all of a sudden I pitch up and crash my bomb into the trees directly on the smoke. Then I pull straight up, spinning. Not that time.

For a moment I feel giddy and am aware of my hands sweating on the stick. For some strange reason I want to see the trucks. But then I think it would be stupid for me to get shot down on my last one. I think about Ben and my moon-faced, yellow-brown whore which I risked a court-martial to take away from a stupid-assed white colonel . . .

I look at my toggles and my fuel gauge. Because she thought I was a confused and fucked-up black motherfucker like Ben. But I wanted her pussy not her sympathy. "Soul-brudder, soul-brudder. I am same-same you."

She came with me and then she found I did not need her love. I just wanted her to walk with me. The finest whore south of Bangkok . . .

I am down almost to the top of the trees and I have forgotten to flip my toggles. I tell Red Dog 1 my toggles stuck and I break away from him and roll over and come across upside down, screaming, then pull up just enough to turn over and let my bomb fly into the orange smoke, and pull up, spinning.

Ben might fall in love with the bitch, and she would fall in love with him. Marry her and take her back to the States and settle down near some nice liberal college and be happy for life. If I wasn't married I would marry her and take her back and have her mess up the mind of anyone I wanted her to mess up the mind of. Give him some pussy if necessary. Pretty bitch. Soft. Loyal. Smooth-skinned. Ah . . .

We cloverleaf and come back across the target for the last time and I think if they don't get me now they never will. If the trees don't open up now they'll never get me.

Forward air controller says: "Number 2, you're too low."

I go lower. Fuck him. I lean forward and look but cannot see, then I tilt to the side and let the last one go and convince myself that I hear metal crash against metal as it explodes, and I climb straight up, past number 1, and the pressure locks me to my seat. It is over. It is over. I laugh until I almost cry.

BEN

This war is like Harvard. Nothing in it is real. Everything seems abstract.

I should have joined the infantry, been splattered with the blood, then it would have been real. This is like Harvard, like death in the twentieth century. The killers never see the killed.

Maum lights another reefer. "I've never seen a person die in this war," I say, but I know she does not speak English. She smiles. Then she frowns playfully because she does not like marijuana herself, but she never complains about lighting one for me. Oriental women never complain about anything, I think. I dry my right hand on a towel on the floor, and take the reefer from her and take a heavy drag. I hold my breath to allow the stuff to soak into my lungs. In the abstract situation I'm in, I can only hate whitey for the smaller symptoms of the disease that he is spreading around the world, like segregating the whorehouses and bath houses over here in Thailand.

Maum lifts my left leg out of the tub and soaps it. Like trying to get the Thai girls to hate Negroes by telling them niggers have tails and niggers have big dicks and will hurt them. Maum drops my leg back into the water. She walks around to the other side of the tub and picks my right leg out of the water and soaps it. She hums a little and smiles. I watch her soft, round, smooth, completely hairless, brown-yellow face, so inward-seeming as if she could teach me things that the narrow gnomic bastards at Harvard could never teach in a million years. If she could only speak my language, or I hers. I shiver for a moment knowing that I must not go back to America with all this hatred in me.

I should never have come into the war, but I came like a sheep. During all my life in America I have been led to loving the wrong things and hating the wrong things like I was nothing more than a goddamn sheep.

I lean forward for Maum to soap my back. I keep on letting myself be led the wrong way because our survival has always depended on our lying to ourselves about . . . But our survival does not depend on that any more. Like I could get shot down, and even the lying will not have saved me.

Maum soaps my chest. "Mass-sagee, mass-sagee," she says while helping me out of the tub onto the massage table. I lie on my stomach. She begins to knead my flesh like black bread dough. I keep my head hanging off the table so I can smoke the fifth reefer that Maum has lit for me.

She has smooth legs and small feet. She pulls herself up on her toes as she kneads the flesh on my rib cage. I watch her little toes grabbing the floor. Then she gets on my back and walks around breaking all the stiffness in my body. Her toes grab my back like they did the floor. I moan a little because it hurts and feels good at the same time. She snaps my arms and legs, then she slides to the floor again while I turn over on my back. She puts a towel over my erected penis. I take the towel off. She blushes. I do not smile back at her. She stops smiling. "Mass-sagee, mass-sagee," she says and takes it in her small yellow hand. I shake my head, no. Then I pull her up on the table with me.

CHILDRESS

The Blue Sky Bar is crowded and loud. My whore and I come into the main room which looks like nothing so much as a long lean-to with a concrete floor and crepe paper streamers hanging from the ceiling. A row of whores sit near the bar. A single light bulb illuminates them as they talk to each other. The juke box, playing Aretha Franklin, glows in the dark near the door. It makes me think of a red-hot, pot-bellied stove. All the corners of the room are dark.

Another small light bulb hangs from a cord near the center of the dance floor. A few black GI's are dancing with whores.

Ben and some friends are sitting at a long table talking shit. I sit down next to Ben. My whore sits across the table.

"Hey," I say.

My whore says, "Hi." She smiles. Her teeth are perfect.

"Lieutenant Childress, Damg. What's happening?" Ben makes a slight bow toward both of us. "So you're finish?" he says to me.

"Yeah."

"I bet you glad."

"That would be a damn good bet," I say. Ben slides his glass across the oilcloth table. I sip. Damg sips. "Scotch. Nice," I say. Ben signals for the waiter to bring two more glasses.

My whore listens to Ben's friends. Ben and I talk, but I listen to what my whore is listening to. A fat darkskin GI says: "That's how the Chucks got ahead of everybody else in the world. Because the average motherfucking Chuck doesn't *feel* anything. He acts like his emotions are dead. I told this white boy the other day: 'At least I have a heart. You don't have one. You've got icewater in your veins. You would kill your own father if the price was right.' "

Another smaller GI added: "I really don't think the white man can feel anything. He acts like his feelings are numb until he gets scared. Then one of them come crying to me: 'You think they coming back?' Talking about the VC. I say: 'Shut up, motherfucker.' We were up near the DMZ. I think that the only time a Chuck cries is when he's scared."

"That's one thing: a brother will cry when he's sad or when he's happy or when he's fucking." one GI says. They laugh.

The GI continues, "A Chuck never stops thinking. He can't even fuck for thinking. He can't dance for thinking. Here he is walking down the street in Bangkok. The nigger is looking at the Thai women, finest women in the world. You hear me: in the world. And he thinks the Chuck is doing the same thing until all of a sudden the Chuck says: 'When the war is over I'd like to buy up some of this cheap property and hold it until the price goes sky high.' " They laugh. "Damn."

My whore says: "Chuck have no love."

Ben looks at my whore. The others keep talking. "Like most of the antiwar motherfuckers. They ain't really antiwar, they're anti-getting-killed-their-damn-selves. A few of them care. But the vast majority of them don't give a damn about these Vietnamese people."

Ben and my whore glance back and forth at each other. I am afraid. I could never live it down if Ben took my whore right from under my nose. Peaches & Herb are singing from the juke box. Ben's legs are moving under the table. I am afraid that he is going to ask her to dance, and they are going to get to talking about that wet-eyed shit, and she will choose to go to the bungalow with him instead of me.

The slow song ends. I relax. The juke box plays:

> I just want to testify
> That you sure look good to me.

I think about the money I have saved during my eleven months in Thailand. In the dim light the Thai girls look like little yella colored girls.

A group of GI's are dancing in a line.

> I just want to testify
> That you sure look good to me.

I feel like I want to join in, but I sit still. Every third beat they stomp and the line slides in the opposite direction. Slide. Slide. Stomp.

Two Thai girls are shoving a huge black sergeant, trying to make him lose the beat. He laughs whenever he double-times and falls back in step. His forearms are like giant smoked ham hocks. He double-times. Stomp. The girls try to pull him off balance. He half-times. Stomp.

> I just want to testify
> That you sure look good to me.

He grins and looks at the ceiling, confident now that he is so into the music that he can stay in step without looking at the feet ahead of him. Half-slide. Long-stride. Stomp. "A-a-a-ah!" He wiggles his ass, spins and slides. Stomp. The two girls continue pushing at him. I look around at the dirty place, at the mis-matched chairs and tables. I think about the matched-up white whorehouses up the row.

Ben is saying something about flying. I am ready to leave. A slow record starts. Ben asks my whore to dance. I grab her hand. "We got to go. I hadn't planned to stay this long."

"Okay. Childress. Damg." He stands up and bows a little toward each one of us and smiles. Some of the others say: "So long." "Peace." "Later."

I hold her hand and rush, almost run outside. The night is cool. I stop a baht-bus.

The boy says: "One man, two baht."

I say: "One man, one baht."

"One man, two baht," he says.

My whore tells him something in Thai. He pouts and accepts the two baht for the two of us.

The air is peaceful as we ride along. Night air blows into the open sides of the baht-bus. The small boy hangs on the rear running board and jumps down whenever the baht-bus stops to pick up other passengers. Each time we have to slide further forward until we are sitting directly against the cab, Damg on one side and me on the other. The breeze is not so strong. I can lean down and look through the rear window into the cab, past the driver and out the front windshield. I decide to take Damg to the luxury hotel that the Americans have built up past the base.

Through the windshield I can see other baht-buses racing toward us down the narrow road between garish little whorehouses with neon signs. They look like all-night, three- or four-lane bowling alleys with tin or thatch roofs. The Hong Kong-made signs: red, blue, green, blinking FLYBOY, THAI HEAVEN, SWEET HOME, YELLOW ROSE, BOOM BOOM ROOM, HONEY BEE, DREAMLAND, THUNDERBIRD.

Further up the road where the Americans are tearing down a mountain to get dirt to build a runway on the sand, the air is full of dust. We are near the base. Three white GI's get off the baht-bus. Dump trucks clog the road. Jet engines whine like wounded animals in the Siamese night.

BEN

The Blue Sky is almost empty. I walk to the rear and ask Papa-san to fix some fried rice for me. Then I walk over and sit on the concrete floor near the well. The other GI's have gone to the bungalows to sleep with their girls, or back to the air base. I do not want to sleep with anyone. My head hurts from too much scotch.

Papa-san watches me while he cooks, but I do not want to pretend that I am cheerful in order to prevent him from feeling sad that I am alone.

He cooks over a small blazing fire in a pan which he never sets down unless to add more ingredients. The food sizzles, and he lets the smoke come up into his face as the small flames lick up from a bed of rocks and touch the bottom of the pan. He serves the fried rice in a wooden bowl. I pay him a quarter. There are large reddish shrimp in the mixture but I do not feel like eating.

"Lieutenant," he says, "Lieutenant."

I smile.

He goes back to the fire, whispers something in the ear of his youngest son and sends the boy off on an errand. I hear the boy running barefoot on the stones outside the rear compound fence. The old man is plum. The faces of his family are lit by the light of the flames. They sit without eating, without talking, for no apparent reason, they are simply there.

The son returns with a thin, youngish girl. Her clothing is wet in spots, which makes it apparent that she has been working in a bath house. Papa-san pushes her toward me, saying: "You sleep with her tonight, Lieutenant."

She takes the last few steps toward me as if she has not lost the momentum from his push. She is a dainty, seventy- or eighty-pound girl with shoulder-length hair and a small mannish shirt covering her pointed teen-age breasts. She tucks her head and blushes. Her shorts are white like the shirt and she has a scotch-plaid belt holding them up. She would look tinier yet if she did not have on high-heel shoes over her white bobby sox. She is amusingly beautiful. Papa-san and his family are happy that I have someone for the night.

"No, Papa-san," I say.

"She no have VD," he says, his voice quickens and rises to assure me. He shows me her card which has a blue circle on it to show that she has passed her last VD inspection. He takes my hand and places it to my ear. I know I am supposed to take wax out of my ear and rub it in her pussy to see if it burns her, but I do not. "I don't want to *pom-pom,*" I say.

The family laughs at the way I say *pom-pom.* The youngest son urges me by slapping his hands together to make the sound that two bodies make slapping together.

The entire family has turned to look at me—four children, a wife and a mother. I hear a transistor radio playing from one of the bungalows.

The girl is embarrassed. "We walk," I say.

"Chi," she says, and the old toothless woman sitting on the other side of the flames shakes her head, yes.

"Yes, *poo ying*," I say.

We leave along the back path in front of the dark wooden

bungalows where several GI's are sitting out with their girls.

The bungalows are in a row like a series of out-houses in back of an old Southern church. A wooden platform runs along in front of them and a naked shiny-skinned GI runs down the platform to where the vat of water is. He squats and washes his privates, then tiptoes back past us into his bungalow.

For a stretch the narrow path leads into the jungle before it turns toward the main road. The girl and I hold hands as we walk along the ditch that carries waste from the tapioca mill down to the ocean. The girl laughs and holds her nose at the wet-dog odor of the ditch. I laugh.

For a moment I wonder what would happen if I disappeared forever into the human and bamboo jungles of Asia.

We reach the road and walk along the stony shoulder. She takes off her high-heels and walks in her sox for a while, then she takes them off too. In some places the air is chilly, and in others we walk through warm air. Walking through ghost, we used to call it down South, before Harvard, before everything became literal and scientific, and then became more unreal than ever it was before, leading straight to Vietnam. Before a million explanations came down between me and what I wanted to feel, and then all the explanations proved to be lies.

As I walk I feel strangely free, and I dread the thought of going back to America. I do not know how I can ever feel right about America again, after what they got weak-assed me to do over here.

I want to go to graduate school, but I know I will never sit in a class and learn from a white man. And who will I work for, and where will I go.

The road turns out of the trees and runs along the beach. The Gulf is empty and the black morning is peppered with stars. The air on the beach is cool. I feel the presence of billions of people around me whose lives are menaced in the same way that my life is menaced. Like the millions of Chinese who were slaves in their own country for centuries.

I think of Damg. I know she understands this, and I know that here, in this small place beside the ocean she is lonely with that knowledge. But just as I could give her an account of the treachery and ambition of the West, she could lead me into Asia so full of endurance like the earth itself. Into Bangkok, Rangoon, Kuala Lumpur, Djakarta, Calcutta and across the Indian Ocean to Africa.

We walk down toward the water's edge. There is nothing man-made in sight except for a puny wooden dock where the trucks come down to pick up the ammunition and jet fuel as it is loaded off the ships anchored in deep water.

"Pom-pom?" the girl says in a weak voice and sits down and begins to undo her shorts.

"No," I say and take out my wallet and give her five dollars anyway. Tomorrow I want to bring Damg on this same walk. We could sit on the edge of this continent which has been kept under the foot of white men, until finally China had to get an H-bomb and say: no more. And the people I am fighting, me, in Vietnam had to say: you can kill me but you can't enslave me any more. And me fighting them. As if my own fate and the fate of American blacks is not linked to the fate of nonwhite people all over the earth.

STACY

The water is cold. I try to turn hot water on but none comes. I get wet gradually and then I do not shiver as the cold water comes down across me. I look through the door down toward where they are building the new runway. Then I see Childress walking toward the showerhouse. He is almost a silhouette against the clear blue sky. I can see that he has civilian clothes on, and that he must be just getting back from town.

He walks slower than usual. But, I think, there is no reason for him to hurry since he does not have to fly this morning.

"Just back from town?" I ask.

"Wheew! Yeah. Walked all the way for a change." He sits down on the shower-house stairs and takes off his shoes.

"Having your last big fling?"

"Yeah. I feel sweaty, funky and drunk." He stands up. "Tonight I'll be in Bangkok. Friday, Hawaii. Sunday, San Francisco. How about that shit?"

"Shit, I wish I was leaving too."

"It takes time, my boy." Naked, he walks up the stairs, turns on a shower and slides slowly under the water. I watch his toes curl up until he gets used to the cold water then his feet relax and flatten out on the wooden floor.

"What about your whore?" I ask.

He laughs slightly. He takes water into his mouth and gargles briefly. He spits. "She's fine. Beautiful as ever with her Chinese-looking self."

"I mean about Ben," I say. "You said you wasn't going to let a Harvard-trained dude inherit the best whore in Thailand."

"I know," he says.

"But there's no way you can stop it from back in the United States, is it?"

The water seems to freshen his appearance. He spits again. There is something frightening about his naked, muscular cleanliness. I step out of the shower and stand on the steps drying myself.

"I hid some communistic papers in her room," he says.

"So?" I stop drying.

"Now all I have to do is call the Office of Special Investigation." He is out from under the water standing in the shower-house door. "When they find the literature, they'll swear that she's a communist. See. And no red-blooded Amurrican, including Ben, will be allowed within a mile of her."

I look at him.

He steps out of the shower onto the top of the stairs.

I feel empty inside.

"It is as simple as that."

"I bet."

"Really," he says.

All I can think of to say is: "You didn't bring a towel to dry yourself."

"I can use yours when you are finished," he says. "I'm not afraid of catching white folk's germs," he says.